LONDON
BLOSSOM

Jackie Wilson

ISBN: 154677422X
ISBN-13: 978-1546774228

DEDICATION

To my daughters, Abby and Chrissy. And to my mom.

CHAPTER 1

May's flight took off at 10:00 p.m. on a warm spring night in Toronto. She peered out the window at the city skyline and the thousands of little lights on the ground as the aircraft flew over the city. Shortly after takeoff, May's mother, Reiko, who was sitting beside her, was fast asleep. May read, watched the news highlights on the inflight screen in front of her, then got up to go to the bathroom at the back of the aircraft. While she was making her way down the narrow aisle, she heard a "psssst" from a small, fiendish-looking blonde girl with a pointed nose and large, crystal blue eyes. The girl looked rather like an elf but without the elfin charm. She was sitting beside her sleeping parents reading a massive book. The little girl, who was scrawny and looked no older than eight or nine, was staring at May with her huge saucer eyes. May, deciding to be friendly, said hello to the girl and asked her what she was reading.

"I'm reading about Iceland in the World Fact Book. I'm Billy."

It took May a few seconds to recover from the fact that someone would name a girl Billy, and she was quite surprised she was as pretty as she was, considering. If the rumour was true that people start to look like their name as they age, Billy was in big trouble.

"Hi, I'm May."

"Nice name," replied Billy.

"Thanks."

May's mother, Reiko, had wanted to name her Jungo, after an aunt who helped look after her when her parents first came to Canada from Japan. The name, meaning child of obedience, appealed to her because May's older brother Gus was a terror and she hoped the name might be a good omen. Thankfully, May was born on the first of May so Reiko decided she would go with the name to please her very British husband, Stanley, who wasn't crazy about his only daughter being named Jungo. Stanley, thrilled with the compromise, insisted May's middle name be something Japanese. Reiko changed her mind about Jungo and went with Bungo, which referred to the classical, literary form of Japanese, a decision that was made after Gus, who was only three, tried to set fire to a pile of books when his new sister was brought home from the hospital.

"It says here that in Iceland, literacy is first-rate by world standards," said the little pixie.

"Sounds interesting," replied May, impressed the young girl was reading about the literacy rates of a foreign country.

"I'm doing a school project on Iceland," said Billy as she pulled up the Global Positioning System on the airplane screen in front of her and pointed out that they were "practically flying over Iceland" on their way to England. May really needed to use the bathroom, so she smiled politely and said goodbye to the young girl.

At the back of the aircraft, she passed her nanny, Petunia, who was sleeping with her mouth wide open. Since May and her older brother Gus, who was now almost eighteen, were too old for a nanny (something Gus reminded his parents of constantly), Petunia's duties were elevated to those of a house manager. She was responsible for cooking meals and making sure everything in the house stayed on schedule. She was unnaturally tall and lanky, so her legs were squished up against the seat in front of her and her head was draped way over the top of her own seat. According to Gus, she looked like she was over a hundred years old, and he spent an inordinate amount of time poking fun at her old-fashioned habits and peculiar behaviour. Every morning, Petunia would read the newspaper standing up, and in the afternoon she would read books about hand-blown glass, even though she had never owned any. When May and Gus were watching television or a show on their computers, she would snap her fingers in their ears and say she was countering the negative effects of the "evil blue screen" by keeping their reflexes alert. Petunia had a collection of plaid wool tights that she wore with thick wool skirts, even on hot summer days, and would use expressions like "horseradish," which Gus tried to explain to her was not translatable to anything in this century. Petunia posted the meal schedule on the refrigerator door on the first of every month, so the family always knew what they would be eating in the coming weeks, taking structure to what Gus called "obsessive levels."

Billy was waiting for May when she walked back, clearly wanting to continue their conversation.

"Have you ever seen the flight deck?" she said as May passed by her seat. "It's where the pilots fly the plane."

"No," replied May. "I thought people weren't allowed on the flight deck anymore."

"Not normally, but my cousin's girlfriend Amy is the flight attendant on this flight, and I've asked her to ask the captain if I can see the flight deck."

"Really?"

"Sure. Do you want to come along?"

There was an empty seat across from where Billy was sitting, so May grabbed her book and sat next to her until Amy came by and summoned them to the flight deck, where the captain greeted them politely. The flight deck was filled with hundreds of dials and buttons, and May was mesmerized by the view. She saw a plane coming in the other direction, and it was only then that she realized how fast the aircraft was flying.

It was still quite dark, but she could see the clouds below and the crimson in the distant sky as they flew east toward the rising sun. At one point, the co-pilot turned around to talk to a flight attendant. With both the pilot and co-pilot facing them, May wondered who was actually flying the plane. As she stared out the front, worried about whether autopilot really worked, she heard the captain raise his voice at Billy in alarm. The little girl had pulled out some sort of device that looked like a TV remote control and was pointing it toward the console in front of the pilot. The captain grabbed the device from Billy and yelled to the flight attendant to come over.

"Amy, can you please get these two young ladies out of here? Do you realize how much trouble I can get into for letting these kids in the flight deck? If she wasn't related to you, I'd land this plane and have her thrown in the slammer!"

"I'm so sorry, Captain," said the flight attendant, looking distressed. "It will never happen again."

Amy shot them the dirtiest look May had ever seen as she grabbed Billy by the ear and dragged her back to her seat. May followed close behind, completely shaken by what had just happened. She wondered what kind of a delinquent Billy was and about the device she had pointed at the pilot. Amy told Billy that she was not to leave her seat for the rest of the flight or else. May assumed that the same applied to her and staggered back to her own seat, shaking. As she sat down, she looked back at Billy inquisitively for some clue as to what had happened, but Billy just looked at her shoes.

May pulled out a London guidebook that her gardener, Zorro, had purchased for her and tried to read it, but the cabin lights were turned off now and she could barely see the print. She didn't want to turn the overhead light on because her mother was sleeping beside her so she gave up on reading and closed her eyes. Despite still feeling slightly traumatized by the ordeal on the flight deck, she was asleep within minutes. Her mother gently shook her awake a couple hours later. May hadn't heard or felt a thing. She opened her eyes to a cabin filled with sunshine as they touched down at London's

Heathrow Airport.

CHAPTER 2

When the numbness from having slept only a couple of hours had worn off, the mortification of having been thrown off the flight deck set in. May cringed when they brought her into the back room reserved for criminals and potential terrorists and questioned her about the device that Billy was using on the flight deck. May was grateful that her mother gave her the benefit of the doubt and defended her vehemently to the airport authorities, insisting that May had never done anything in her life that even came close to breaking any rule. The authorities decided that May was an innocent bystander and let her go with a warning to be more careful about who she associates with in the future. She wasn't sure what was going to happen to Billy, but her mom said that they were analyzing the remote control device and were pretty sure it was really only a TV remote. Apparently when Billy had pointed the device at the captain, she had told him to land in Iceland so she could do some first-hand research for her school project.

It was almost noon when they headed to the East End of London, where they would be staying with Petunia's sister Bertha, another last-minute change from the modern chic hotel Reiko was supposed to have stayed at with Stanley before the plans were changed. May felt pangs of excitement infused with fatigue as she looked out the car window at the unfamiliar landscape during the long drive across the city. The houses looked old, charming, and completely different from the ones in her suburban subdivision in Toronto.

Bertha lived in a pretty little townhouse surrounded by a wine-coloured brick wall overgrown with thick vines. She had a tiny front walkway and a little porch beside the entranceway. Several people were standing around the front of the house and swarmed the car as soon as it came to a stop. When May opened the car door, there were offers to carry her bags, questions about how the flight was, and inquiries about how she was doing from people she didn't know. A portly woman with a very red face made her way through the crowd, walked straight to Petunia, and hugged her. Petunia introduced the portly woman as her sister Bertha.

"I've always called her Barty," said Petunia. "But most people call her Auntie Bart."

May thought Bart and Barty were the strangest nicknames she had ever heard and started to wonder whether Billy was such a bad name after all. Auntie Bart grabbed May and her mother and gave them bone-crushing hugs. Unlike her tall, skinny sister, Barty had a short, stocky build and looked like someone who might be good at throwing a shot put. May also thought she looked about forty years younger than Petunia even though she knew they were close in age.

"Thank you so much for having May," said Reiko.

"It's the least I can do. You've been so good to Petunia," said Auntie Bart as she led them through the small kitchen to the back of the house and outside, where several more people were standing around eating and drinking from a picnic table in the middle of the backyard.

"The neighbours wanted to meet the folks from overseas, so we decided to have a party. You must be half starved!" she said as she walked over to the picnic table. The backyard was long and narrow and covered with the most magnificent and interesting plants and flowers May had ever seen, which was saying a lot because Zorro was a talented, prize-winning gardener. There was even a huge palm tree in the middle of the lawn, which May found strange.

"Your garden is out of this world, Auntie Bart. What's your secret?" asked Reiko.

"I watch *Gardening with Flowerz* with Penelope Flowerz every week. I never miss it. She's fabulous. Do you watch her in Toronto?"

"Yes—she's wonderful. Petunia tells me she's coming to the neighbourhood to tape a live show."

"Yes. She'll be filming here in the East End on Monday. She's introducing her new show, *Penelope's Pastries*. If she can do with pastries what she has done with gardening, everyone in England will be as fat as cows."

Petunia and Auntie Bart giggled simultaneously in the exact same manner, and although they looked nothing alike, there was an uncanny similarity between them when they laughed. May and her mother couldn't help but laugh along with them.

"Reiko, I'm sorry that your vacation with your husband was ruined," said Auntie Bart as she scooped a mound of potato salad onto her plate.

May resented the general sentiment that her mother's vacation was *ruined*. After all, at least half of the time she was to spend here was for business.

"What happened to your poor husband?" asked Auntie Bart as she made a sandwich.

"He got a bad ear infection a couple days ago," said Reiko. "It was serious enough that his doctor recommended he not fly, as there was a chance that he could lose some of his hearing."

"Oh, that's too bad," Auntie Bart said.

"I know. Stanley was really looking forward to visiting several sites before we were to reconnect after my conference; the Imperial War Museum and the Churchill War Rooms... you know, all the things I'm not interested in."

"Well, it's a wonderful opportunity for May to see London," said Auntie Bart.

"When the airline gave us the opportunity to transfer the

ticket, I thought May would love London. And who better to show her around London than Petunia," said Reiko.

May looked at her mother in disbelief. That was not exactly how May remembered it happening. The ticket was originally offered to Gus, but his hockey team had made the playoffs and Gus was the star goalie. After Gus turned down the opportunity, May overheard Petunia trying to convince her parents that it would be a good learning experience for May, offering to be her guardian. The trip happened to fall on the week between classes and final exams and May only had two exams this year, in subjects in which she was at the top of her class. Although Petunia's argument was convincing, several hours passed before an offer came. May suspected that her parents thought the vacation would be wasted on her. The family had been on two resort vacations to the Caribbean in the past few years, and while everyone else seemed happy to partake in all the activities the resort had to offer, May was happy to sit in the shade and read her book. Gus attempted to convince her to try sailing, waterskiing and scuba diving, but she was content sitting back and watching as he dominated the beach volleyball tournament, snorkeled, and won a limbo dance contest at two in the morning. Although she was having a perfectly good time, her parents seemed frustrated with her lack of participation. But London was no beach vacation. She was interested in exploring the city that was the setting for so many of the novels that she loved, written by the likes of Charles Dickens and Sir Arthur Conan Doyle.

"When will you be back from your conference, Reiko?" asked Auntie Bart.

"Tuesday night."

"We'll take good care of May until then."

As May finished eating a sausage roll, she looked up and saw a tall, slim boy with auburn hair, freckles, and a bony face sitting on the brick wall at the back of the garden with a book in his hand. May thought he looked around the same age as Gus as he peeked through the crowd mischievously. As the lunch commotion died down, he shot May a friendly but inquisitive smile, stepped down from the wall, and walked toward her. When he reached her, he offered her his hand and gave a slight bow. "Please allow me to introduce myself. My name is Chester T. Yorke. Welcome to England. Home of the British monarchy."

May was thrown off by Chester's formal manner. She curtsied as she shook his hand and with a bright red, flushed face replied, "I'm May B. Abbott. I am very pleased to meet you, Chester." Then she curtsied again.

Chester's head flew back in a loud laugh and he had to lean on a nearby chair for support. "Unbelievable. A curtsy. Willow will love that one."

May stared at the boy, perplexed and embarrassed.

"I'm sorry," he said. "I'm just teasing you. I was just trying to emulate my good friend Willoughby. He's a really old-fashioned bloke. His formal introduction always seems to throw the women off balance. I've been practicing keeping a straight face for months. I wanted to see what reaction it would get out of a Canadian girl."

"How did I do?" said May sardonically, still feeling heat in her cheeks from embarrassment.

"Fantastic. Very nice curtsy," he chuckled.

"Thanks," she said self-consciously.

Chester suddenly looking like he felt a little guilty said, "My friends call me Chet, by the way. Is this your first time in London?"

"Yes."

Auntie Bart came out with a big tray of desserts and offered them to everyone. As she reached May, she said, "I see you've met my grandson." She called May's mother from across the lawn. "Reiko, have you met my grandson?"

May's mother made her way over. "So this is the great nephew Petunia's been telling me all about?" she said, shaking Chet's hand.

Chet turned to May and whispered, "No curtsy from your mother. How rude."

May laughed, finally feeling her embarrassment dissipate.

Chet led May to the far end of the garden to sit on a large, multicolored hammock, picking up several more pastries from his grandmother's picnic table along the way.

"This is such a great backyard. Do you come here to visit your grandmother often?" asked May.

"I actually live here with her. Just until school is over. I'm from Sheffield."

May noticed that Chet's accent was considerably different from Petunia's and Auntie Bart's.

"My father wanted me to attend school in London this year so we could spend more time together," continued Chet. "He moved back here when my parents divorced. I grew up in Sheffield with my mum. Dad was a musician and wanted me to pursue music at the same school he attended. I was supposed to have lived with him, but he passed away just a few days after I received my acceptance letter. We were both looking forward to spending time together, because we hadn't lived together since I was very young."

"Oh. I'm so sorry," said May.

Chet had a soft, gentle manner that put her at ease. "No, I'm sorry. I know that's sort of personal. I don't usually talk to people about him. And since I've only known you about three minutes …."

"No, that's fine. I'm a pretty good listener. I've had a lot of practice with my brother, Gus, and my gardener, Zorro."

"Zorro?"

"Zorro's our Hawaiian gardener. He does the gardening for most of the people on my street. He loves to talk, and his surfing stories are legendary. Only to be outdone by the stories my brother Gus tells about whatever trouble he's been in."

"Ah, the infamous Gus. We've even heard about him over here."

May and Chet exchanged stories about their hometowns as they sat and ate cakes and pastries. May was surprised how easy it was to talk to him and was glad there was someone close to her age, since everyone else in attendance seemed to be Petunia's age. When they headed indoors, they found Reiko providing Auntie Bart and Petunia with information about where she could be reached for the next few days. While they sorted out contact details at the kitchen table, a boy popped his head into the living room. He was tall, with a muscular yet lean build and had the blackest hair May had ever seen, which stood straight up from every angle. He had pale white skin and was dressed all in black. Around his neck was what looked like a leather collar with silver spikes on it. Large safety pins held his torn T-shirt together in several places, and he wore large black boots with silver buckles that came up to his knees. He had large spacers in both ears and tattoos all down the back of his neck and his left arm.

"Hello, Sidney," said Auntie Bart. "Come on in."

"Hi, Auntie Bart. I tried to knock but no one answered."

Sidney reached over and gave Auntie Bart a kiss on the cheek, and she gently patted his cheek back.

"Would you like something to eat, Sidney, love?"

"No, thanks. I already ate at Hammer Dog's house."

Auntie Bart frowned. "Hammer Dog is not an appropriate way to refer to your uncle, dear," she reprimanded.

Sidney ignored the comment and said with what May detected as sarcasm, "Am I interrupting something?"

"No, of course not," said Chet, stepping in with introductions. "Sid, this is my great-aunt Petunia, Mrs. Reiko Abbott, and her daughter, May."

Auntie Bart cut in and continued the introduction. "My sister Petunia has been living with May since she was born. They live in Toronto. Well actually," she clarified, "in the *suburbs* of Toronto."

"The *suburbs*..." said Sidney, leaving the word hanging. That time there was no doubt of the sarcasm, but May seemed to be the only one to notice. Sidney gave them a polite nod then turned to Chet. "Chet, I'm just picking up that piece of music."

"It's in my room. Come on up."

The two boys ran upstairs and came back a few minutes later.

"Chet, we're practicing a little early tonight, so come by

Hammer Dog's... I mean Uncle Hamilton's right after dinner."

"I know. Uncle Hamilton already told me."

"Come as early as possible, because I have to leave at nine o'clock for a meeting."

Chet shot Sid a reproachful glance, which May picked up. "That's fine, Sid," he said. "I need to get back here early anyway to study for an exam."

When Sid left, they all sat down to tea in the living room, where Petunia and Auntie Bart exchanged old stories and local gossip. A while later, May rubbed her tired eyes as she watched Chet scurry out the door with a piece of cake in one hand and a small instrument case in the other.

"See you later, Grandma," yelled Chet as he walked out the front door.

When he was gone, Auntie Bart explained to May and Reiko that Chet would be heading back to Sheffield in three weeks when exams were over. Reiko nodded politely but May could tell that she wasn't really listening and had been preoccupied by something since Sid's departure.

"Auntie Bart," Reiko asked. "Does that Sidney boy come over often?"

Auntie Bart, sensing the reason for her concern, replied, "Oh, don't let Sidney's appearance worry you, Reiko. He's a very good boy. He's quite a musical talent and very intelligent. He plays jazz with Chet when he's not wasting his talents playing the most horrible rock music imaginable with his band. I know he studies really hard and..."

Auntie Bart's defence of Sid was cut short by an old man who walked into the room wearing thick pajamas with penguins on them. His hair was as white as snow and was slicked back on top and curled under at the bottom where it sat on his shoulders. Auntie Bart got up from the table and put her hand on the old man's back.

"Did you have good nap, Bedrich? You slept for half the day!"

"Did I?" said the old man.

Auntie Bart introduced him to everyone as her husband,

and he sat down beside May.

May's mother, undeterred by the interruption, insisted on continuing her inquiries about Sid. "I can't imagine any parent allowing their son to get so many tattoos."

"We've never met his parents. He lives with his uncle Hamilton. Chet tells us Hamilton was a great jazz musician. We see him at the school meetings. He's a nice enough fellow."

"How does a boy like that afford to go to that school?"

"Mom!" cried May, embarrassed by her mother's insensitive comment.

"I don't know. I'm sure he manages to pay somehow. Maybe Sidney is on a music scholarship like Chet."

"I wonder what kind of home life he has to have to live with his uncle," said Reiko.

May was starting to feel embarrassed by her mother's lack of tact.

"Sid's all right, Reiko. Not everyone can have a good home life. He's in a good school and Chet says he is extremely bright," said Auntie Bart affectionately.

"Hmmm," said Reiko, looking like she didn't believe a word. "But the way he looks! He's so…unhealthy looking. When do you think he last ate a fruit?"

"Hard to say. I try to feed him fruit when he comes by. Awfully pale," said Auntie Bart.

"Do you think that's his natural hair colour?" said Reiko.

"I don't know but someone painted that boy's arm while he was asleep," said Bedrich.

May's mother had told her that Bedrich had gone "a little funny" in the past few years, saying outlandish things.

"Those are tattoos, Bedrich," said Auntie Bart.

"Well whatever they are, if I find out who did that to the poor boy…" replied Bedrich.

They heard the front door open and saw Chet run toward a desk in the living room. He reached into one of the drawers in the hall and pulled out a music book.

"Forgot this. Oh hi, Grandpa," he said, noticing Bedrich.

"Hello, my dear boy."

As Chet ran out and closed the door behind him for the second time, Auntie Bart leaned in and whispered, "The story is that when Uncle Hamilton's wife died, he never played in public again. He was a real talent once upon a time. Chet's learned a lot from him."

Bedrich looked at his watch and said, "Bertha, it's almost seven."

"Oh, yes." Auntie Bart turned to May and her mother and said, "I don't mean to be impolite, but Bedrich and I have got to watch Penelope Flowerz. You must watch it with us, Reiko."

"Actually, I think I'm going to turn in early. I have a car picking me up early tomorrow morning."

"Why so early on a Saturday?"

"There's a luncheon and golf tournament tomorrow for guests of the conference. I'm entertaining clients."

"And what about Sunday. More golf?" asked Auntie Bart.

"I need to prepare for Monday's presentation on Sunday."

May was also tired from the travelling and decided to pack it in as well. As she followed her mom up the stairs to the guest bedroom she would occupy for the week, a hush fell over Auntie Bart's family room.

"*Welcome to* Gardening with Flowerz, *with your host, Penelope Flowerz. This week, Penelope attempts to grow orchids in Alaska!*"

"*Hi! I'm Penelope Flowerz. This Monday I'll be hosting my brand new show called* Penelope's Pastries, *live from my old neighborhood in the East End of London! Tickets are sold out but you can win them by logging onto my website at www.penelopeflowerz.com.*"

May put her head on the pillow and was soon falling asleep to the fervent and rather annoying voice of Penelope Flowerz.

CHAPTER 3

The next day Chet made an appearance for breakfast while May and her mother were studying the schedule they had worked out for May's first day in London.

"Take a look, Chet," said Reiko. "May and I did extensive research and believe we have an agenda that even a Londoner would appreciate."

Reiko, an accountant and senior partner at a top consulting firm, was used to planning for success and had a somewhat smug look on her face.

Chet took a look at the day's agenda and smiled. "It's certainly thorough," he said, sounding sincere, though May noticed a slightly raised eyebrow.

Thorough was the magic word for Reiko, and she breathed a satisfied sigh of relief. There was a loud knock at the door and Reiko gathered her suitcase. "That will be my ride."

She turned to May with a nervous smile and said, "I'm sure you and Petunia will have a wonderful time. Make sure you stay close to her and don't forget to input Auntie Bart's number and street address into your Dad's phone in case you get separated."

Reiko had made May leave her own phone behind because

she said she didn't want to pay for international data and her dad already had a plan from work. But May knew her mother thought she'd sit in her room and chat with her friends the whole vacation if she had her own phone.

"Don't worry, Reiko, I'll take good care of her," said Petunia.

"Yeah, don't worry, Mom. I'll be fine."

"And don't use the phone unless you really need it."

"I won't."

She wasn't going to put her contacts into her father's phone. Besides, Auntie Bart didn't even have internet at home so she was unlikely to use it at all.

Everyone hugged Reiko and wished her a good few days at work, then May walked her mother out to the car and said her goodbyes. When she came back into the house, she overheard Auntie Bart asking Chet if he wanted to join them on any of their touring.

"I've already asked him," said Petunia.

"I'd love to, Grandma, but they didn't leave any time to breathe in that schedule, and I'm afraid I might suffocate from overscheduling."

"I believe they are a detailed bunch," said Auntie Bart.

"There has to be an element of spontaneity whilst travelling," said Chet.

May, who was still standing in the doorway unnoticed, cringed at Chet's comment. It reminded her of a conversation she'd had with her brother the night before her departure for London. She had been sitting on her bed reading a book after taking a last look at the contents of her suitcase when Gus knocked on her bedroom door.

"Hey, sis. What are you reading?"

"Shakespeare's *Twelfth Night*," replied May.

"What's it about?"

"It's about this girl Viola who gets shipwrecked, pretends to be a man, but then falls in love with the duke who she's working for on the island."

"So this duke dude thinks she's a man?"

"Exactly," replied May. "Meanwhile the duke sends Viola to talk to Lady Olivia, who he's in love with, and Olivia falls in love with Viola."

"Pretty progressive for Shakespeare's time."

"Not really. Viola is dressed like a man, remember? Try to keep up."

"Doing my best, sis, but my brain shut down as soon as you said the word *Shakespeare*."

"Anyway, at the end..."

"Wait...how do you know the end if you're only halfway through the book?" asked Gus.

"I've read it before," she said.

"Of course you have," said Gus, shaking his head in disbelief. "So what happens at the end?"

"You'll have to read it yourself," said May.

"Not in my lifetime," he laughed, throwing a pillow at her.

May threw a pillow back at him, which narrowly missed his head and landed on her dresser. "Get lost, Gus. I want to finish this before I go to bed. Viola's just about to reveal she's not a man."

But instead of leaving, Gus sat on her bed and gave her a long, serious look. "Actually, that's kind of what I came here to talk to you about."

May giggled preemptively, thinking he was about to tell a joke, but his face remained serious. When she realized there was no joke forthcoming, she began to feel a little uncomfortable. She was not used to Gus being serious.

"What's up?"

"Listen, I know you love reading, and that's great, but I don't want you to be the kind of person who lives her life in a book," he said gravely.

May was perplexed but didn't respond, still surprised by his serious tone.

"You spend a lot of time reading about and listening to other people's stories but you never go out and experience things yourself."

"Are you going to bring up the beach vacation again? This

is not the same. I'm actually looking forward to this vacation."

"You'll be going to university in a few years, and you are pretty *innocent.*"

May looked at Gus in frustration. The term *innocent* bothered her more than she could explain. Her friends thought she was innocent as well. The same friends she'd been hanging around since she was five. They all lived on the same street and had grown up together, but for some reason, things had begun to change over the past year. Two of them had boyfriends now and had started keeping things from her. She couldn't understand why. She was *not* that innocent. She lived with Gus! How could she be innocent?

"What I'm trying to say," he continued, "is that I think your itinerary is a little too structured."

"Mom says I thrive on structure," she answered defensively.

Gus looked at her and sighed. "Forget about what Mom says for a second."

He looked like he was struggling with what he was trying to say.

"Try to let loose a bit and have a good time. Try new things. Get lost in the streets of London one day. It will give you a little more—" he hesitated "—experience."

"Hey, I'm *experienced* in theory, having listened to you weasel your way out of trouble all these years."

"It's not the same thing. Just try to be a little spontaneous."

"Don't worry, there will be plenty of room for spontaneity," said May, feeling a little annoyed.

"May, there is barely enough room on that itinerary to take an unscheduled bathroom stop."

"Come on. It's not that bad."

May didn't mention that Zorro had given her the same lecture right before dinner. She had to admit that the schedule was really full, but there was so much she wanted to see, and she felt it had to be planned very carefully. She didn't want too much time to wonder about where to go and what to do.

As Gus got up to leave, he pulled out a small white

envelope and handed it to her. "Just think of this as an early birthday present, in case you need it."

"My birthday was a month ago."

"Whatever."

May opened the envelope and pulled out several large notes of British pounds. She looked at the bundle of money and said, "This is a lot of money. Mom already gave me and Petunia plenty of money to do all the things we've planned."

"I want you to have it. To do something *unplanned*. I'm sure you'll find something worthwhile to spend it on."

May looked down at the envelope and then up at her brother.

"Now finish reading your boring four-hundred-year-old story," he said with a smile.

"Thanks, Gus."

"No worries, sis."

*   *   *

So they all thought her plans were overscheduled, including Chet. May coughed so Chet, Auntie Bart, and Petunia would realize she was standing in the doorway.

Surprisingly, her spirits weren't dampened by everyone's concern. After Chet left, she walked out and sat in the rocking chair in the front walkway with her itinerary and purse in hand, elated about embarking on a day in one of the world's most fascinating cities. Unfortunately, her excitement did not last very long. Petunia and Auntie Bart left to go to the grocery store to allegedly pick up some snacks for the trip into London but didn't return for two hours.

May walked out to meet them on the street as they returned and overheard them giggling about how they were going to see Penelope Flowerz on Monday. She hoped she had misheard, because May and Petunia were supposed to be going to the British Museum and several other places on Monday. She was becoming anxious because they had already missed two items on their tour list during the time Petunia and Auntie Bart were at the grocery store.

"I think we should get going now," said May politely, trying to control the concern in her voice.

"Oh well, we're just going to enjoy the garden for a bit and then we'll head out later."

Head out later? thought May. *LATER?* She again tried to keep her voice calm and said, "Oh...but we're already really behind schedule. We're supposed to be at the Tower of London right now...at the place where Ann Boleyn got beheaded."

"Seen it lots of times before," replied Petunia.

May was incensed. Where was the lady who kept all her activities on schedule and who made sure meals were like clockwork? Petunia seemed to have her own ideas about what a vacation in London should be.

"You're not missing much, dear," interjected Auntie Bart. "You'll hear a lot of stories about a bunch of dead people."

A bunch of dead people? thought May, outraged.

"We'll try and squeeze it in tomorrow, May. Why don't you just enjoy a non-scheduled day for once," said Petunia.

May wanted to ask what the aliens had done with the real Petunia but felt helpless and dejected. She was thinking about the fish and chips place that Zorro recommended, where they were supposed to go for lunch. She opened her guidebook and sat in the rocking chair on the tiny front porch. Today she would be missing Westminster Abbey, a place that would be closed tomorrow, as it always was on Sundays. Several famous British people were buried there, including Queen Elizabeth I and her notorious half-sister Mary otherwise known as Bloody Mary. She had promised her dad she'd look for Sir Isaac Newton's burial place and she'd promised Zorro that she'd check out the commemoration for Dylan Thomas, his favourite poet. May herself wanted to see Charles Dickens' tomb because he had written some of her favourite stories, including *A Christmas Carol,* of which she owned six different film versions, including the musical.

The day was warm and breezy, and she closed her eyes for a

few minutes as the sun warmed her face. A wave of fatigue washed over her, likely due to the jet lag, and she nodded off with her guidebook in her lap. She woke up suddenly when she heard the front door close. She looked up, and wondered who had gone into the house. The sun was now behind the clouds and she felt a slight chill. She put on the sweater that had fallen off the chair while she was sleeping and rubbed the sleep out of her eyes. She could no longer hear Petunia or Auntie Bart and was wondering where they were when Sid came through the front door.

"You're up," he said.

May jumped up with a start, sending her guidebook flying off her lap and onto the ground. "Yes. I guess I fell asleep," she replied, feeling embarrassed.

Sid was wearing a tattered black shirt that said *Fugazi* on it. He wore his signature high-buckled boots, but his hair was less spiked than it had been the previous evening.

"Are you planning on sleeping the whole time you're in London?" said Sid dryly.

May was taken aback by the insinuation. "No, of course not," she said defensively. "Actually, I should be at Westminster Abbey right now. It's just that Petunia's been...busy with other things."

What was she supposed to say?

"I'm kind of stuck here," she added, suddenly feeling like she had to explain.

"I see," replied Sid. "Can you not just go by yourself?"

May was perplexed by his question. She felt her face burning and figured it was turning a bright shade of red. She was a sixteen-year-old in a large, strange city and didn't know how to get to Westminster Abbey by herself! Why was he asking her these questions?

"Well, I just got here and don't know the city too well," she said dejectedly. She felt like a provincial bumpkin in front of Sid, who seemed like such a denizen of all things cool and urban. Although she had lived her whole life right outside one of the largest cities in North America, she had rarely made it out of her large suburb, a fact she was starting to question and regret. The moderate sense of humiliation was escalating to a crescendo that threatened to burn her face right off.

"What's at Westminster Abbey that interests you, May?"

He remembered her name.

"Well… um…" There were so many reasons she wanted to see the great cathedral, but she went with the first one that popped into her mind. "Charles Dickens is buried there."

"I see. So you like Dickens?" Sid shot her a half smile and May felt like she was on trial.

"Yes, I love him."

"What about Shakespeare?"

"He's not buried at Westminster Abbey," replied May, feeling disproportionately triumphant at her answer.

"I wasn't asking you if he was buried at Westminster Abbey, I was asking you if liked him."

Smartass.

Sid's eyes twinkled mischievously and the smile he cracked was just enough to show a perfect set of white teeth. May felt her pulse suddenly pick up.

"Yes, I love Shakespeare," she whispered, feeling slightly aggravated. Or feeling slightly something she didn't quite recognize.

"And you're right. He's not buried at Westminster Abbey."

"I know," May said softly, confused about how fast her heart was suddenly beating.

"Many tourists think he is," grinned Sid.

"Well, I guess I'm not your typical tourist," retorted May, surprised at her saucy answer. Why was she talking like this? She didn't even know where that tone had come from. She wasn't sure why she was letting this freakish boy get under her skin.

"Well, enjoy yourself when you finally get to Westminster Abbey," Sid replied softly, sounding a little more genuine, though May suspected that the tone might be in the pity range.

"Thanks," she said as sincerely as she could muster.

She returned to her guidebook when Sid left and read about

the Houses of Parliament, which were across the street from Westminster Abbey. The famous clock at the Houses of Parliament was called Big Ben. Zorro's guidebook said that Big Ben actually refers to the largest bell, which weighs fourteen tons. Twenty-eight thousand pounds. *How interesting*, thought May, outraged that she was reading about places she could be visiting. After seeing Big Ben, the plan was to walk up the street to Whitehall, the building of the horse guards, and see the changing of the guard. Zorro's guidebook said that they were supposed to be guarding the Queen, but May knew that the Queen's permanent residence was at Windsor Castle, where Her Majesty spent most of her time and where May was scheduled to visit with her mother on Thursday.

May wondered what Gus was doing and missed him for the first time since leaving. She wished he was here and wondered what he would do in this situation. She reckoned he would just hop on a bus and tour the city by himself. But May couldn't fathom doing that, so she just sat on the front porch all afternoon staring at her guidebook, feeling stranded. She could hear Auntie Bart in the backyard telling Petunia about how she had purchased the tickets to see Penelope Flowerz months ago. Every giggle hurt May's ears. It was the most frustrating afternoon of her life, knowing that all the wonderful places she was reading about were so close.

As the sun embedded itself in the western sky, and May was gathering her things to go inside, Auntie Bart came onto the front porch and said, "Chet has offered to take you out for an ice cream."

An ice cream? Sure, an ice cream would replace seeing the tombs of Queen Elizabeth I and Charles Dickens.

"Sure," she said instead, feeling defeated.

Chet came outside a few moments later and smiled at May. "So I hear I'm taking you out for ice cream."

"You don't have to. I'm enjoying myself. Really," she lied.

Chet looked at her and laughed. He reached into his pocket and pulled out a small object in the shape of a credit card, which he placed into May's hand.

"What's this?"

"It's a Travelcard for the Tube," said Chet.

May had read about the Tube in her guidebook and knew it to be the London subway.

"It's good for all the buses as well. It'll get you anywhere you want to go."

"Thanks," said May. "Where are we going?"

"Into the city, of course. I can't guarantee *Westminster Abbey*…"

"How did you…?"

"Sid just called. He said I was being a rotten host."

May felt a tinge of humiliation at the thought of Sid. He had called Chet to save the helpless suburbanite who wouldn't go into the big city by herself. Just the thought made her cringe. The fact that it was true made her feel even worse.

"Chet, you don't need to…"

"I was heading into town anyway. I'd love some company."

May was sure he was lying but wasn't going to refuse an offer to get her out of earshot of Petunia's laugh. She didn't think she could stand another story about Penelope Flowerz, who she was starting to dislike immensely.

"I don't think I can convince Petunia to let me go downtown without her."

Chet gave her a confident gaze. "Let me do the talking."

They walked through the house to the backyard, where Petunia and Auntie Bart were sitting drinking something deep burgundy with fruit in it.

"I'm supposed to be at rehearsals downtown in an hour, and I thought May might enjoy seeing the play."

"That's a brilliant idea," said Auntie Bart.

Petunia sat up sternly and looked at her sister.

"They'll be fine, Petunia," she said reassuringly.

Chet turned to Petunia and said, "We'll come straight home afterward."

"Well, I suppose that would be all right," conceded Petunia. "Have fun at the play. I used to be quite a little actress myself when I was in school," she added wistfully.

May couldn't believe that Petunia would allow her to go into the city without her or any other adult. What would Reiko say? It seemed Petunia didn't care at the moment.

So May and Chet headed down the tree-lined street together, Travelcards in hand.

CHAPTER 4

Chet and May hopped onto the Tube, which was a few short blocks from Auntie Bart's house. May pulled out her itinerary from a small backpack and Chet let out a giggle.

"Don't laugh!" said May. "I'm just looking."

Still, she couldn't help but laugh along with him.

"Okay, let me see it again," said Chet.

As he perused the well-organized document, he quipped that it looked more like a novel than an itinerary. "I'll see what I can do," he said, handing it back and looking down at a vintage watch on his wrist.

"You said you have to be at a rehearsal?" asked May.

"I'm supposed to drop off a hat at the Globe Theatre after five."

"The *Shakespeare* Globe Theatre?"

May had read about the Globe Theatre, an open-air playhouse that showcased Shakespeare's works.

"Yeah. Some kids from my school are rehearsing for a play there. Me and Sid are helping out with some of the costumes and props for the play."

Chet opened a leather bag he was carrying and pulled out a flat velvet hat with a large feather sticking out of a brooch at the side of it. "I picked this up yesterday at a specialty costume store."

"Nice," said May. "Why are they practicing at the Globe Theatre?"

"Our school and a girls' school get together to do a play every year. We're doing it at the Globe this year because we're performing for several members of the royal family on Saturday. I'm pretty sure the Queen is attending."

May looked at him strangely.

"You're joking, right?"

"I'm not joking. I know how crazy that must sound," said Chet. "I couldn't believe it either when I found out. I sometimes forget the incredible privilege afforded to those who attend this school."

"Wow. It must be amazing to go to such a prestigious school."

"It's an education we can't really afford, so I feel pretty lucky."

"So how do you pay for it?"

It was a question May would normally have withheld. In fact, she would have been mortified had someone else asked it, but she felt such a sense of goodwill and sincerity between herself and Chet, even in the short time they'd known each other, that the words just came out.

"I have a small trust fund that my dad left me, and a music scholarship."

"Your mom must be really proud."

"My mother thought I wouldn't fit in there because our family doesn't have the kind of money or status that most kids in the school have. She was wrong, though. It's never been an issue. It helps to be best mates with Sid, I suppose. Not having money doesn't seem like something he's all that worried about. Plus, he's really popular with the blokes. They think he's uber-cool because he's in a great punk band that is starting to get some publicity. Not to mention that no one would ever mess with him."

They got off the Tube beside the cathedral that May recognized as the one Princess Diana and Prince Charles were married in. St. Paul's Cathedral was right by the River Thames, and they walked across the street and onto the Millennium Bridge. Before stepping onto the bridge, Chet stopped and looked back at the cathedral.

"St. Paul's was rebuilt in the seventeenth century by Sir Christopher Wren. He's one of the greatest architects to come out of England," he said.

"Oh," said May, not knowing who Christopher Wren was because she'd skipped over the architecture section of the guidebook.

"I love architecture," added Chet. "Christopher Wren also did Kensington Palace, which I can take you to as well. There's a great café there called the Orangery."

May slowed her pace as she crossed the bridge to try to take everything in, looking over the railing at the boats below and at the interesting buildings along the banks on both side of the river. She felt a rush of excitement as she took note of her surroundings. She was mesmerized by the modernity of the Millennium Bridge. It looked as if it came out of a futuristic London. But despite the imposing concrete and grey steel wires, it seemed delicate, subtle, and even whimsical.

"This is a really cool bridge," she said in awe.

"It's the first one we've built across the Thames since the Tower Bridge was built in 1894."

Although May didn't know much about architecture, she guessed that the evidence of the bridge's genius was the fact that it didn't seem out of place among the older buildings and bridges that surrounded it.

"It was built to commemorate the millennium in 2000," Chet continued.

At that moment she understood for the first time that reading something in a book wasn't the same as experiencing it, an assertion Gus had been making for as long as she could remember.

"It's amazing," she whispered.

Chet pointed out the Shakespeare Globe Theatre on the other side of the bridge, a plain, white, stucco building that looked like it belonged in a different century.

"It looks just like I'd imagined it," said May.

"You may have seen pictures of it in your guidebook. It's a replica of the old Globe Theatre from 1599."

May was impressed by Chet's knowledge of dates, facts, and the history of everything.

"It has the only thatched roof in London," he said.

"Right," said May. "What's a thatched roof again?"

"Looks kind of like a straw hat. Made of straw and moss. You see them on some of the beautiful traditional pastoral homes in pretty English towns. There's a bylaw in London preventing thatched roofs because they're a fire hazard. The theatre got special permission to put one in so it would look just like the old one, but they had to put in a sprinkler system. In fact, a fire is what destroyed the first Globe Theatre."

May laughed.

"What's so funny?" asked Chet.

"I was just thinking of something my brother, Gus, did last week, when you mentioned fire."

"Petunia talks to Auntie Bart at least once a month, so we hear the stories at the dinner table. He likes to throw off the equilibrium of an otherwise perfectly organized house, right?"

"On a daily basis. My mom's an accountant and my dad's an engineer," she said in their defence. "They like things structured."

"Really? I never heard that," said Chet with a sarcastic smile.

May conceded with a little chuckle.

"So what did Gus do this time?" asked Chet.

"He burned down the neighbour's shed and half of her fence. He was mixing some liquids, a few of which he 'borrowed' from his lab at school, to create some homemade fireworks."

Gus had been caught in the previous couple weeks for a series of offences May's parents called "appalling and delinquent." When the police called, Gus had to endure the same confused look on his parents' faces they always had when a teacher or the principal of the school called to let the Abbotts know that he was in trouble. Reiko and Stanley claimed that they both came from a long line of professionals and intellectuals and that their gene pool was "sound." So when Gus got into trouble, they would stare at each other dumbfounded and say things like "Do you think Gus's genes have mutated somehow?" or "Do you think we picked up the wrong baby from the hospital?"

May tried to explain that Gus was just curious, adventurous, and in dire need of stimulation. She was sure he felt restless and confined by the structure of his school and home life, and might perhaps have developed a certain mischievous spirit as a result. May covered for her brother whenever she could and was always rewarded by Gus's wonderful capacity for making his outings sound even more exciting and interesting than they actually were. He would sit on her bed when he returned from whatever he had been up to, sometimes waking May up very late at night, to entertain her with descriptions of what he described as "healthy excursions."

Before they continued across the Millennium Bridge, Chet took several pictures of her with the Globe Theatre in the background. The wind blew through the bridge cables, and it began to rain lightly. They started running to avoid getting wet, past the main gates of the theatre and around to the main entrance on the left side of the building, where they bumped into a few students who were standing around outside the doorway. Chet greeted several of them before he spotted Sid in the piazza and headed toward him.

"Hey, Sid. How's everything going? Has rehearsal started?"

"No. They're kicking us out. The cast of one of the real plays needed some last-minute rehearsal time. They're letting us come back to rehearse after the exhibit closes tomorrow at five p.m."

"Too bad," said Chet. "I wanted to pop in and show May the theatre."

"They just shut the doors," said Sid.

"Okay, we'll try again tomorrow."

May wondered whether Petunia would come to her senses by then.

"Where are you two headed?" asked Sid.

"I think I'll bring May over to Trafalgar Square. If we have time, we'll pop into the National Gallery."

"It closes soon, so you better hurry," said Sid.

They all walked back over the Millennium Bridge together toward St. Paul's Cathedral. It had stopped raining as suddenly as it had begun, and the sun was trying to peek through the dispersing clouds. Walking beside Sid, May felt her face tingle with the residual embarrassment of her afternoon humiliation.

"Sid, why don't you come along?" said Chet. "We can walk May up to Soho for a bite before we head back."

"I have to be somewhere at six."

"Somewhere…"

'Yeah, somewhere."

"I see," sighed Chet, looking at Sid skeptically.

Sid stopped and faced Chet as if he was waiting for him to say something. It almost looked to May from the way they were standing that one of them might pull out a sword and challenge the other to a duel, but then Sid turned quickly and started walking eastward. From over his shoulder he said, "It was nice seeing you again, May."

May just waved awkwardly, still flustered.

Chet stood for several long seconds and watched Sid walk away before heading west toward Trafalgar Square. He was clearly disturbed by something and was silent for several minutes as they headed down the busy street. The walk was long but interesting and when Chet broke the silence, he pointed out landmarks and shops along the way. By the time they reached the National Gallery it had been closed for a half hour, so they sat in Trafalgar Square, where May admired the Nelson Column, the large fountain, and the statues that surrounded the square. They stayed for a while to watch the many street performers playing to the tourists before heading north to Soho.

The pretty neighbourhood was lined with cafés and

restaurants. Chet took May into a cozy little tearoom and ordered them both some tea and sandwiches. It was obvious to May that he was still irritated by what had taken place earlier and was trying to hide it by making light conversation.

"Chet, is everything okay? You seem a little preoccupied," said May, finally succumbing to curiosity.

"You noticed. I'm sorry," he answered.

"First of all, no need to apologize. If it wasn't for you I'd be watching last year's reruns of the Penelope Flowerz show with Bedrich right now."

May put some milk and sugar into her tea and placed her plate of sandwiches on her lap. "It sometimes helps to talk about things," she said. "I listen to my brother's exploits almost every day. Nothing could surprise me. Trust me."

Chet looked at her inquisitively as though trying to determine whether he should confide in her. Then his face softened and he said, "I'm really worried about him."

"You mean Sid?" asked May.

"Yes. He's been acting very odd lately."

"In what way?"

"I first noticed it about six months ago. He started to become quiet. He used to be passionate about several environmental causes. He'd ask everyone to sponsor him for events that were taking place to raise money for environmental awareness. He'd rant about politics and the environment and I'd tease him about his diatribes. I could see that he was becoming a little disenfranchised by what he called the 'diplomatic' process but I never thought anything of it. It was around the same time he met this guy called Diego at one of his environmental meetings. After that, everything stopped. The ranting. The diatribes. He stopped talking about causes that were important to him. He just became really withdrawn. Then the silence turned into brooding. He's been angry and short-fused ever since, and I've noticed his music has suffered."

"Who is this Diego guy?" asked May.

"He's apparently the leader of a new extremist

environmental group. Diego's philosophy is that in order to be heard, you have to take radical measures. Six months ago, a science lab in the city was blown up. Diego didn't take credit for it but the press has been following the story really closely and suspect that Diego was responsible. Then two months ago another lab that creates a highly toxic pesticide was set on fire."

"Why would Sid want to join a group like that?"

"Sid's cousin, who was a farmer, died of cancer last year. Sid took it really hard. They spent a lot of time together as kids and were like brothers. I think Sid was looking for answers and was probably pretty impressionable at the time. Diego convinced Sid that the products his cousin used on his crops caused his cancer. In fact, truth be told, recent studies have proved just that."

"That's terrible."

"I know. But Diego's methods aren't any better than those of a terrorist. I asked Sid if he was involved in the fire a couple months ago and he didn't give me a straight answer. He's become so secretive. When I question him about anything he shuts down. He refuses to discuss anything relating to Diego or his group with me. I'm scared he's gotten involved in something that's way over his head."

"Does anybody else know how Sid's been acting?"

"I've told Willoughby, but he's not much help. There's a bit of a rivalry between he and Sid. It's strange. They're friends, yet they're constantly at each other. It's hard to explain."

"Who's Willoughby again? Is he the old-fashioned guy who you imitated to get me to curtsy?"

"He's the one."

"How about someone in Sid's family like his uncle Hot Dog?" she asked. "Maybe he could talk to him."

"It's Hammer Dog," laughed Chet. "I've thought about that, but if I go running to Hammer Dog, Sid might see that as a betrayal and that might alienate him further."

May got up, ordered two slices of carrot cake, and brought them back to the little table.

"Does Sid have any other family?" she asked, handing Chet a fork.

"He occasionally mentions his mum but never in any detail. His family is from the Isle of Wight, which is a couple hours south of here."

"Is that why he stays with his uncle while he's at school?"

"I guess so. I have no idea."

"Isn't he a good friend of yours?"

"I'd consider him my best friend. He's a year older than me so when I started going to this school, he really took me under his wing. He even lets me practice with his band occasionally. But blokes don't talk about that stuff."

"Oh."

"I mean, we talk about some stuff. We both lost our dads, so we've kind of talked about that."

"Well, hopefully you're wrong about the radical stuff and he's just going through some sort of phase," said May.

"I hope so."

They finished their cake and headed back to Auntie Bart's. May looked at her watch and wondered whether Petunia would be worried about where they were but when they got back to the house, Auntie Bart and Petunia were sitting at the kitchen deliberating about where they should go shopping the following day. May wasn't sure what they thought she was going to do by herself for the next few days, but before she could contemplate her unfortunate circumstances, Chet turned to his grandmother and said, "Why don't I bring May to rehearsal again tomorrow. I can also show her around town some more."

Petunia and Auntie Bart exchanged what May interpreted as relieved looks. They had obviously not resolved the conundrum of what to do with May while they were busy enjoying themselves.

Later, when everyone was in bed, May quietly knocked on Chet's bedroom door.

"Come in."

May peeked in and Chet gestured for her to enter. May

stepped into a large but cozy space where she found Chet sitting cross-legged with an acoustic guitar in his lap on a sofa covered with several plush cushions in rich, dark shades. Beside him was a large bookshelf and a stand with a small turntable on it, presumably to play the boxes of vinyl albums that were lying around the floor. The walls were adorned with music and art paraphernalia, most prominently a large poster of a young Miles Davis in New York.

"Great room," said May.

"Thanks."

"You really don't have to look after me tomorrow. It was really nice of you to offer but totally unnecessary."

"Don't be ridiculous. I liked hanging out with you today. It was like discovering the city again for the first time. You should have seen your face today on the Millennium Bridge. It was priceless. Plus, I have the distinct feeling from looking at *THE LIST*..."

"What list?" May said playfully.

"The *don't-leave-time-for-anything-impulsive-or-you-might-spontaineously-combust* list. Sound familiar?"

"Never heard of it," she laughed.

"You need to lose the list and let loose, May. Go with the flow. Let your hair down."

"So you think I'm uptight?"

Chet looked at her good-naturedly. "Actually, after spending the afternoon with you, I think you're pretty easygoing."

"I don't have much of a choice at the moment now, do I..." said May.

"Good point," laughed Chet.

"I'll see you tomorrow then," said May, closing the door behind her.

"See you tomorrow, May."

CHAPTER 5

The next morning Petunia and Auntie Bart left early to go shopping, and May and Chet headed toward the city to do a little touring. May promised to leave the list behind for one day and just check out some of the sights without a strict agenda. They planned to get to the Globe Theatre around five-thirty just after the class began to rehearse. They started the day at the Stock Exchange and Bank of England buildings, then moved on to several other London landmarks before heading to the bustling shops in Covent Garden. After an afternoon of walking around and listening to Chet's history of London, which she thoroughly enjoyed, they walked down toward the Thames, where they again traversed the Millennium Bridge in the late afternoon. It was too early to go the Globe Theatre as it was still open to the public so they visited the Tate Modern art gallery just next door, where they had an early dinner. May used some of the money Gus had given her to treat Chet at the Tate's renowned seventh-floor restaurant, which provided an excellent view of the city. They lost track of time and arrived at the Globe a half hour behind schedule.

May was eager to see what the theatre looked like inside and was not disappointed when she walked through the doors. It had an authentic sixteenth century atmosphere and May felt as though she had been flung back to Shakespearean times. The stands were circular and made of wooden benches, where students were sitting and chatting quietly while watching the action on the stage. The theatre was round and looked like a miniature stadium with an open roof. She looked up at the sky and marvelled at how uncovered and unprotected the venue was, wondering what happened when it rained during performances. May and Chet made their way to the front row, where Chet sat beside some students who were watching rehearsals. In front of the stage was an open area called *the yard* where, during performances, people could stand and watch the play.

In the middle of the yard looking up at the stage stood a tall, dishevelled woman with long, curly brown hair wearing far too much makeup. She was directing the action on the stage.

May took in the drama as the students practiced their lines and the dishevelled woman barked directions, looking like she was overwhelmed.

"This might be a bit boring for you," said Chet.

"Not at all. I love Shakespeare," said May. "And I LOVE *Hamlet.*"

"How did you know it was *Hamlet?*"

"We did a production last year at our school, so I recognize it. Our drama teacher is really cool. He had us do a modern version that was set in New York. I helped with the lights."

"Set in New York?"

"Yes—he got the idea from a movie."

"How did it turn out?"

"It was great. The modern setting helped students relate to it a little more."

"I think *Hamlet* would be fantastic set in any era, in any city. A murdered father, a corrupt uncle, a mother with questionable morals, insanity, betrayal…need I go on?" said Chet.

The students were dressed in regular clothes except for the boy who was playing Hamlet. He was clad in full Shakespearean attire, black tights and a velvet crimson jacket buckled up at the waist.

"So these are the kids from your school?" asked May quietly.

"Not the girls."

"Of course. I forgot you go to an all-boys school."

"Actually, there aren't too many girls' parts in the play anyway. The main ones are Gertrude, who is being played by Kate, and Ophelia, played by Hannah. The rest of the girls are just playing background parts."

"Is Kate one of the professors?" asked May, noticing she was much older.

"No. Kate is a famous stage actress."

"Really?" said May, not recognizing her. "Why is she in the play?"

"Every year we do a big production where we try to get a well-known actor to come in and be in the play with us. Instead of them telling us about their experiences onstage, we actually get to work with them. Watching their process and acting with them is an amazing opportunity."

"Wow. What a great idea. It's too bad more of the girls can't be in the play."

"They haven't complained much. Just watching Kate work is a great experience. Plus, they are doing another production at their school in a couple weeks."

"If you love *Hamlet* so much, why aren't you in the play?" asked May.

"I auditioned," said Chet. "I thought my audition went really well. Professor Winterbottom told me I was excellent and had cast me in the role. The next thing I knew, Tucker Wilde was playing Hamlet and I was on the costume committee."

May tried to stifle a laugh and Chet looked at her.

"Winterbottom?"

"Yes, she's the drama teacher at the girls' school and is directing the play. That's her up on the stage. I guess it is a rather humorous name."

He *guessed*? Only in England would you find a name like

Winterbottom, thought May.

Chet looked at the boy in full costume. "Apparently his father pulled some strings. He donates a lot of money to the school."

"Oh. I'm so sorry, Chet," said May.

Chet shrugged and looked up at the stage toward Tucker. "It's alright. It's just as fun to watch it." But he didn't sound convinced. "What about you, May? Why weren't you in your New York version of *Hamlet*? You seem to be as big a fan as me."

"I would never be able to stand up on a stage in front of a crowd. I'm more of an observer," said May.

She was too embarrassed to tell Chet that she had learned every line of the play after Gus encouraged her to try out for the role of Ophelia. He always was encouraging her to break out of what he called their parents' "unhealthy mold." She had practiced with Gus every night for a month but couldn't even work up the courage to try out. Gus was furious with her.

May and Chet sat and watched for a while as different students took to the stage. Professor Winterbottom's makeup was deeply smudged as the sweat poured down her face. She looked frazzled and worn as she paced back and forth.

"Stage LEFT, MR. WILDE. STAGE LEFT!" she hollered.

The boy dressed in full Shakespearean attire spun around and took a bow. "Yes, m'lady."

The whole class laughed.

"That is quite enough, Mr. Wilde. I'm glad your antics are entertaining the class today, but do you realize the play is in less than a week?"

"I do indeed, my fair, fair, professor."

The boy again bowed low to Professor Winterbottom, who looked furious, and again the students laughed. May thought his antics were funny and laughed as much at how out of place he looked in his velvet jacket and black tights.

"Why is Hamlet in full attire but the rest of the class isn't?" asked May.

"That's because Tucker Wilde is a veritable git."

40

May didn't know what a git was but assumed it wasn't good.

A tall, stocky boy wearing a large bowtie and a pinstripe jacket came down from the stands and greeted Chet. His brown hair was slicked back and he had thick, round, reading glasses on that made him look like he was a New York stockbroker from the 1920s.

"Chet, old chap, what say you?"

"Hey, Willow," replied Chet.

"What a load of rubbish Tucker is. I can't believe you're not up there instead of that lout," Willow sneered in a decidedly Scottish brogue.

"It doesn't really matter, Willow," said Chet. "When are you rehearsing your scene?"

"Not for a while, so I thought I'd see what was going on here."

The boy in the pinstriped suit was staring at May curiously as he spoke.

"Willoughby, this is May Abbott. She's from Canada."

"Bloody nice to meet you, May Abbott from Canada. I'm Willoughby McGregor from Scotland."

"It's nice to meet you, Willoughby," May replied, staring at his bow tie, wondering if there was another play going on.

Chet put his hand on Willoughby's shoulder and said, "I tried imitating you when I met May just to throw her off. She'll never be the same, poor thing. I even got a curtsy out of her."

"A curtsy? Well done, young Chester. I knew you had it in you," said Willoughby.

Chet turned to May with a sardonic smile and said, "Please excuse Willoughby; he was born in the wrong century."

Willoughby ignored Chet and addressed May. "So have you had the chance to see much of London yet?"

She found his Scottish drawl a little hard to follow.

"Just a bit," she replied.

"Has Chet told you the whole history of the city yet? He likes to educate people with his great historical knowledge. You can see the girls yawn from miles away when he's telling them about the Royal Society."

Chet raised an eyebrow and smirked.

"Try not to bore the Canadian guest, please, young Chester," said Willoughby, slapping Chet hard on the back.

"I actually thought it was quite interesting," replied May sincerely.

"See Willoughby, some girls are actually interested in learning something useful and might not want to hear about the latest dog racing results."

Chet told Willoughby about the modern version of Hamlet that May had described.

"That's bloody extraordinary. *Hamlet* is a very ambitious play for a high school," said Willoughby.

Chet grimaced and said, "Not sure if you noticed, Willow, but *we're* doing *Hamlet*."

"Yes, but we attend one of the finest schools in England. You don't find this kind of education anywhere."

"You're starting to sound like Tucker."

"That's *not* funny. Do *not* compare me to that scoundrel. I do not take advantage of the privilege that has been afforded me. Look at him with his tights on. Bloody ridiculous."

Willoughby was speaking loudly enough that a chorus of "shhhhhs" was thrown his way from all over the theatre.

"*Hamlet* is ambitious, but we're also not exactly being one hundred percent faithful to it either," Chet reminded Willoughby. "They cut it down again. It's two one-hour halves now."

Willoughby turned to May and whispered, "Please, May, tell me about your modern version."

Willoughby's manner and old-fashioned way of talking really did make it seem to May like he was lost in a time warp.

"Our teacher got the idea from a movie version that was set in New York," said May.

"Bloody brilliant. A lot more interesting than this stale bunch of oafs. Hamlet's mum is looking a little like Hamlet's grandmother, wouldn't you say?"

"I thought you were thrilled to be working with Kate," said

Chet.

"I am. Too bad this is her last day!"

"What?"

"Haven't you heard? She's starting rehearsal for a play in New York. Leaving tomorrow."

"Who's going to replace her?" asked Chet.

"Winterbottom, I reckon."

While the students were taking a short break, the boy in Shakespeare attire walked over and stood by the bench where they were sitting. He was looking rather sour when he noticed May.

"Who the devil are you?"

"I'm May," she replied, slightly bewildered.

"Are you here to interview for the fan club job?"

Chet and Willoughby looked at each other and burst out laughing.

"Did you start your own fan club, Tucker?" said Willoughby.

"One member strong," Chet chuckled.

"He does one advert and he's trying to start a fan club for himself," said Willoughby incredulously.

Professor Winterbottom shot them a dirty look, and they were asked to keep their voices down by students who were close by.

"She most certainly is not here in the hopes of running your phony fan club, Tucker," said Willoughby. "May is visiting Chet's family from overseas and it's none of your business who she is. In fact, she was just telling us about how her school did a production of *Hamlet* last year set in New York before you rudely interrupted her. Please continue, May," demanded Willoughby turning his back on Tucker.

"How ridiculous," cut in Tucker, still standing there looking proud. "Nothing like corrupting Shakespeare with a setting on the wrong continent. I wouldn't expect anything more from Americans," he scoffed.

Willoughby and Chet exchanged annoyed glances.

"I thought our version was rather clever," retorted May,

surprised at her courage.

"Perhaps if your audience is learning impaired," chortled Tucker.

"Since when are you such a Shakespeare purist, Tucker?" scowled Willoughby. "If you weren't cast in the play, I'm not sure you'd even know who Shakespeare is."

"I'll have you know that my *Macbeth* paper won third prize in last year's essay contest."

"Can't even buy a first prize, Tucker?" sniggered Willoughby. "You might want to get someone more expensive to write your paper next time."

"Sod off, you little twit."

"Please excuse us, Tucker," said Willoughby. "I'd like to hear the end of May's story. I'm sure she was just about to tell us about someone with *talent* playing Hamlet."

Tucker turned to walk away and Chet said, "By the way, her accent is Canadian, Tucker, not American."

"Whatever. Better than your common accent."

Chet lunged toward Tucker and Willoughby jumped to restrain him, thwarting his attempt to punch Tucker by a fraction of an inch. Two boys who were close by jumped up to help Willoughby restrain Chet. Professor Winterbottom, who was talking to some students, turned around when she heard the commotion.

"What's going on over there?" she said sternly.

"Nothing, Professor," answered Willoughby as Tucker scurried away. May was staring at Chet in disbelief. He was so gentle and cultured; she couldn't believe she had just seen him try to punch Tucker in the face. Chet noticed May's look and said, "That's the way we handle gits like Tucker in Sheffield."

"Don't let him get to you, Chet," said Willoughby, putting his hand on Chet's shoulder and gently sitting him down on the nearest bench.

Chet, changing the subject immediately said, "Did I miss the part where Hamlet's father's ghost comes out of the trap door?"

"Yes—they messed it up again," chuckled Willoughby. "A

couple people almost fell into the hole again. They forget it's there."

May noticed that in the middle of the stage was a large, square trapdoor where actors could pop up from underneath the stage.

"This is a pretty sorry production. Tucker the talentless playing the lead role and Kate is leaving tomorrow."

"I know. It's a bit of a nightmare," laughed Chet.

"And here comes the other nightmare," sneered Willoughby.

His nightmare was an extraordinarily pretty girl with long, straight black hair who was walking out onto the stage. She was tall and slim and had a pale translucent hue and naturally red lips. Chet's disposition changed dramatically as soon as he saw her. He ran his fingers through his hair and started fidgeting. Willoughby, noticing Chet's sudden restlessness, said in a disgusted voice, "Ah, please tell me you've bloody well gotten over her. I don't know why you bloody bother."

It seemed to May that Willoughby liked to use the word *bloody* an awful lot.

"Quiet, Willow, I'm trying to listen."

Willoughby rolled his eyes and turned to watch the scene. Chet looked on with a slight smile on his face as she recited her lines in a sweet and mellifluous voice.

"I shall th'effect of this good lesson keep,
As watchman to my heart. But, good my brother...um..."

The girl hesitated.

"Oh, bollocks," cried the boy who was playing Laertes.

"Watch your language, young man," cried Mrs. Winterbottom

"But she never knows her lines," protested the boy.

May leaned quietly over to Chet and Willoughby and whispered,

"Do not, as some ungracious pastors do,
Show me the steep and thorny way to Heaven."

They both looked at her, impressed.

"Ms. Frost," cried Professor Winterbottom. "The line is, *Do not, as some ungracious pastors do, Show me the steep and thorny way to Heaven.*"

"Yes, yes. I'm just distracted by all these people," the girl blurted out, her voice sounding considerably less sweet.

"There will be fifteen hundred people watching you next week!" cried Professor Winterbottom. "Distracted by a few of your fellow students? Goodness me! And don't just stand there, Ms. Frost, show some emotion," she implored.

"Oh no, there goes the hair," said Chet.

Professor Winterbottom's curly hair started to flare outwards. It began to look like a huge ball surrounding her head, and it was now sticking straight out like the mane of Frankenstein's bride.

"What's happening to her hair?" asked May.

"When she becomes angry, nervous, or frustrated, her hair just gets frizzy. It will actually start standing straight up. Defies gravity," said Chet.

"No one can explain it," added Willoughby.

"Wow," whispered May. "That's amazing."

Hannah closed her eyes as if trying to muster up water from a dry well and chanted in a loud but choppy and uneven voice, "DO NOT...... AS SOME.... UNGRACIOUS PASTORS DO......SHOW ME.... THE STEEP.... AND THORNY WAY TO HEAVEN."

Her eyes were closed as she moved to the front of the stage. She uttered the last words with affected emotion and arms spread, then she swooped sideways, tripped on her long, flowing shawl and fell off the stage.

CHAPTER 6

There was a collective gasp from everyone in the theatre. Several students ran over to her, including Chet, who was one of the first to reach her.

"Hannah, are you hurt?" he asked as he knelt down beside her.

"Of course I'm hurt, you idiot," said Hannah.

Chet looked wounded by her words as Professor Winterbottom arrived and cried for someone to call an ambulance. Willoughby turned to May and whispered, "Hmmm, so she *is* human. I thought she might have smashed into a million pieces when she fell off the stage. As my mum always says, what goes around comes around. *Steep an' thorny way to heaven* indeed," laughed Willoughby. "Bloody brilliant."

The paramedics came to take Hannah away and Chet went with her to the hospital. On the way out the door he grabbed May by the shoulders and asked her if she still had her Travelcard, to which May nodded.

"I've messaged Sid. He's going to come pick you up and bring you home. He said he'd be here shortly."

Willoughby stepped in and offered to take May home, but Chet told him that Sid was planning to come by the theatre anyway and pointed out that Willoughby lived in the West End of the city, while Sid lived in the east just a few blocks from Auntie Bart's. After the ambulance left for the hospital, Winterbottom roamed around the theatre in a frenzy, talking to herself.

"First Kate, then Hannah. No Gertrude and no Ophelia. It's catastrophic. CATASTROPHIC!!! Will I have to fill in for Ophelia as well? Oh, my hair!"

Winterbottom's hair now resembled a dust ball from the Wild West. Willoughby, who had returned with May to sit on the wooden benches beside Professor Winterbottom, stood up suddenly and said, "May knows Ophelia's lines. She can fill in for today until you find a replacement for Hannah." May turned white with terror and felt as if she might faint. The tips of her fingers started to tingle and her mouth was dry. She was furious with Willoughby for bringing any sort of attention to her.

"Oh, no. I absolutely couldn't. I've never been on a stage and I don't really know how to act."

"You'll do great, May," said Willoughby encouragingly.

"No. You don't understand. Like I was saying to Chet earlier, I'm more of an observer. I like to watch the drama unfold from afar. Like…really, really far."

"Oh, you have an American accent!" Professor Winterbottom said in dismay.

"She's Canadian," said Willoughby.

"Well, never mind. No time for a fuss," said the professor. "Let's get to it, young lady. We don't have all day. Her Majesty will be watching this play in six days, Ms….."

"Abbott," replied May.

Professor Winterbottom put her arm around May and led her onto the stage. May's feet felt like lead as the professor dragged her up the stairs. She stood frozen for a long time. She wanted to explain to everyone that this was a big mistake. She was just visiting. She wanted to lie to them and tell them that she really didn't know the lines after all, but she couldn't get the words out. Every eye in the theatre was staring at her inquisitively, skeptically, curiously. Her heart was beating so furiously she could feel the pressure of blood pounding against a vein in her neck. Her breathing grew rapid and uneven, and she started seeing stars. She knew she was hyperventilating and tried to deliberately slow down her breathing.

She had seen Gus hyperventilate on purpose once, so she knew the symptoms. He had been practicing for a presentation he was doing in front of the class. He said if you breathed fast enough and deep enough, you would lose consciousness due to the decrease in carbon dioxide in the bloodstream. Of course, he was glad to demonstrate. First he would get lightheaded and dizzy. Then he would become as white as a ghost. Then right after telling May he was seeing stars, he would pass out. May though it quite amusing, but Ms. Grimm, Gus's grade twelve teacher, was furious at what she called a "dangerous and imprudent spectacle." When Ms. Grimm phoned their mother that night, she added that the sort of attention-seeking Gus was engaging in was "gravely unhealthy" and recommended a psychologist.

"May?"

Willoughby was suddenly standing next to her, looking worried as the blood disappeared from May's face.

"May, just recite the lines the way you did a few minutes ago. Chet and I thought you were brilliant."

May stared blankly at him. Everything was spinning and going black. Willoughby put his hands on her shoulders and whispered, "Be not afraid of greatness: some are born great, some achieve greatness, and some have greatness thrust upon them."

Willoughby's flair for the dramatic infused something comical into the situation and May felt a little blood return to her cheeks as the words of Shakespeare gave her a momentarily reprieve from her dire situation.

"*Twelfth Night*, right?"

"Affirmative," smiled Willoughby.

May closed her eyes and tried to slow her breathing. *You are brilliant*, she mumbled to herself. She repeated the words in her head. *Brilliant*. Gus had always told her she'd eventually have to come out of her shell. Something stirred within her. If Gus could do it, she could. They were, after all, from the same family, weren't they? *Some people have greatness thrust upon them.* Well, maybe not greatness exactly, but it was a start. She opened her eyes and started walking toward the middle of the stage, where Tucker was standing looking smug. She could feel his eyes burning into her. Her shoes were loud on the floor as she walked. She looked up at Tucker with all the courage she could muster and said, "Let's start with Act 3, Scene 1, after Hamlet's 'to be or not to be' soliloquy…uh…can I just see the script for a second?"

"Professor Winterbottom!" protested Tucker. "She doesn't even go to your school. She's from another country."

"Mr. Wilde, I don't care if she's from Mars. Have I mentioned there are six more days left before the performance?"

Tucker cleared his throat and suddenly looked a little nervous. He handed the script to May without saying a word, and she fumbled with the pages, landing upon her line, which she showed Tucker.

"Ophelia enters and Hamlet says, *the fair Ophelia,*" she said, pointing it out for him. "Just until Claudius and Polonius enter," she said tentatively.

"Fine! *The fair Ophelia. Nymph in thy orisons. Be all my sins remember'd.*"

He said the lines robotically and rolled his eyes as he looked at her, waiting for her line, but her momentary courage dissipated as she met his cold gaze. Perhaps this wasn't the perfect place to start to come out of one's shell after all. She tried to open her mouth but couldn't. Instead of hyperventilating, she was now not breathing at all. She stepped backward, precariously close to the edge of the stage. She needed to run away. She knew the line but couldn't say it. Her mother had taken a public speaking class once where they told her that statistics showed that the number one fear of most people is speaking in public. Death was number two.

Her face was burning. For an instant, she had thought she

could do it. Turned out she couldn't. Her legs wouldn't move, so she was stuck on the stage. She was utterly paralyzed. Bewildered. Defeated. She looked at Tucker for what seemed to be a lifetime. He glared back at her impatiently then gave her the most arrogant look she had ever seen.

"Okay, I've had enough of this rubbish," he said and started walking off the stage.

As May looked at him departing, she heard a sound. She looked around to see where it had come from, but all eyes were still on her, and Tucker had stopped and turned back toward her. It took her a couple seconds to realize that *she* had made the sound. She never did figure out what triggered it. All that stuck with her was seeing Tucker walk away. This was the boy who had taken the role from Chet. He hadn't earned the role. His father *bought* it.

"What did you say?" asked Tucker.

"*How does your honour,*" she whispered.

"SPEAK UP, MS. ABBOTT," yelled Winterbottom.

"HOW," she squeaked loudly. "Sorry…" she said, lowering her voice. "*How does your honour for this many a day?*"

The words came out in a choppy manner, but once the first couple lines were out, her tone began to steady and she was able to finish the scene. She knew it wasn't *brilliant*, as Willoughby had predicted it would be, but she felt a sense of pride for finishing.

The room was completely quiet and May stood there awkwardly until Professor Winterbottom said, "I've never heard Shakespeare with a Canadian accent. How dazzling. Very avant-garde. Her Majesty will love that an exchange student is in our play. I amaze myself with my own brilliance. It certainly needs some polish, and let's face it, you'll never be a great actor, but I liked the long pause at the beginning of the act. It created a certain amount of tension."

May was again speechless and didn't respond as Winterbottom handed her the week's rehearsal schedule. She slowly walked off the stage and over to Willoughby, who was waiting for her with his arms spread out, ready to hug her. May was so stiff, however, that when he tried to put his arms around her, they ended up bumping heads and he awkwardly patted her on the back with both hands. He recovered quickly from the clumsy moment and said teasingly, "Such a seemingly normal girl able to play someone who's going insane so well. Highly disturbing,"

"It *is* a little disturbing," said May, only half joking.

"Tucker's parents have spent a fortune on acting lessons and you outshone him," said Willoughby.

"That's very nice of you, Willoughby, but Professor Winterbottom said I couldn't act."

"She says that about everyone. Take it as a compliment. If she really thought you couldn't act, her hair would be standing up again."

May thought that having observed characters like Petunia and Gus her whole life was her version of going to a famous British performing arts school.

She looked down at the schedule that Professor Winterbottom had handed to her, then turned to Willoughby. "I thought I was just filling in for today. I can't spend all this time in rehearsal. I have all these things planned."

"We'll figure something out. I'll talk to Winterbottom. It's too bad, though, because you were bloody brilliant. Bloody brilliant indeed."

May blushed deeply.

"That'll do, Willoughby. Quit badgering the tourists," said a voice from behind them.

They both turned to find Sid standing there.

"Chet called me and asked me to take you back to Auntie Bart's house." Then he turned to Willoughby and said in a mocking voice, "Smashing tie, McGregor."

Sid's voice was guarded, quiet, and low even when he was joking.

"Thank you, Sidney," replied Willoughby, ignoring Sid's tone. "I just had it custom made."

"So what happened to Chet?" asked Sid.

"Hannah fell off the stage and Chet went to the hospital

with her. I think it's despicable the way he caters to that wretched girl. You should talk to him about it," replied Willoughby.

Sid ignored the comment and started walking toward the exit, motioning with a nod for May to follow.

"Sid, I could have taken May home," said Willoughby, following them toward the exit.

"Have you ever even been to the East End, Willow? Are you sure you'd be safe there with that tie?"

Sid's eyes were bright and mischievous. He seemed to enjoy his own sense of humour. Willoughby looked down at his tie, brushed off the comment, then looked back up at May.

"May, it has been a great pleasure meeting you. You're such a lovely and fascinating young lady."

Sid shook his head in disbelief.

"Bye, Willoughby." May waved as she walked with Sid toward the exit.

"And you have such talent," he added, following them to the exit. "And a delightful accent."

At this last comment Sid stopped and turned toward Willoughby with a sardonic yet somewhat fond smile and said, "Are you quite finished with your eighteenth-century courting ritual, McGregor?"

Willoughby looked undeterred. "Okay, cheers," he said as Sid and May stepped onto the street outside the Globe Theatre.

CHAPTER 7

May and Sid walked together in complete silence. She glanced over at him several times, waiting for him to say something, but he didn't say a word.

"Thanks for taking me home," she said, deciding to break the ice. "I'm not sure I'd remember how to get back."

Sid ignored the comment and kept walking, staring straight ahead.

"The water looks really nice at this time of the evening," she continued, trying to make small talk.

"Hmmm," said Sid coolly.

May's parents had always said that when there was nothing to say, it was best not to fill the silence with small talk or what her father called "nonsense," a sentiment that May was uncomfortable with. The only time she was comfortable with silence was with her mother and father. Although she didn't always know what to say to fill the silence in social situations, it was rarely necessary, having been surrounded by talkative people her whole life. Her two best friends were in the debating club at school and talked non-stop. Gus fashioned himself a modern-day Odysseus and talked incessantly about his "legendary exploits," and Zorro told stories almost daily about catching the perfect wave in Hawaii and his strategies for winning first prize in the Bloom on the Street contest for the fourth year in a row.

May tried to start a conversation a couple more times while they were walking but Sid replied with one-word answers. She wondered whether he was upset about having to come get her. Perhaps he had been in the middle of doing something important. When they got to the other side of the bridge, Sid stopped and checked his watch.

"Are you hungry?"

"A little."

"Me too."

They walked west toward Trafalgar Square. May was still a little uncomfortable but decided that whatever Sid's reasons, she would respect the fact that he was obviously in no mood to talk. Or maybe he just didn't want to talk to *her*. She got the sense from their first conversation that he disliked her, and now perhaps she was unconsciously trying too hard. They walked for a while then hopped on a bus for a few minutes that took them to Trafalgar Square. Sid led her to a charming church facing the square that she hadn't noticed the day before. He brought her through a side door, down some ancient looking stairs, through an archway, and into the basement, where there was a gift shop and café. They stood in line and both ordered some soup and a tea, still without saying a word, and sat down and ate quietly. May was fascinated by how medieval the place felt. On the floor were tombstones built right into the ground.

They finished their soup and walked up the stairs to the chapel, where Sid put some money in the donation box and escorted May to one of the back pews. At the front of the church was a small choir singing. May had never heard anything so beautiful. She wondered what they were singing, and as if Sid had read her mind, he said, "Bach's Magnificat. The acoustics are incredible in this place."

Sid sat perfectly still, concentrating on the music with an intense expression. His piercing blue eyes looked almost fierce, and May could feel the intensity of his breathing beside her. It made her so nervous, she could feel her own breathing becoming more rapid. His gaze softened as time passed, as if the music was influencing his mood. She glanced over at him surreptitiously and saw him closing his eyes. His face looked tranquil and peaceful and his skin was white and soft-looking. Suddenly he looked at his watch and got up without saying a word. May followed him out of the chapel. They started walking back east along the Strand. May did not know where they were headed but she had a feeling they weren't going back to Auntie Bart's house.

"Um…" said May, unsure how to asked him where they were going.

Sid stopped and turned toward her. He looked into her eyes as if contemplating something and then inhaled a deep breath.

"I just need to run a quick errand before I take you back. It will just take a few minutes. Is that alright?"

"Yes, of course."

After walking for what seemed like a long time, they came upon a large group of picketers demonstrating in front of a building. There were several people with signs and T-shirts that said "Stop the Insanity," "Where's the Justice?" and "The Earth has no Voice." Sid looked at his watch and went to sit on the steps of a building across from the picketers. They were chanting "This must stop" over and over.

May sat down beside Sid awaiting an explanation, but he didn't provide one. As workers in the building came out, demonstrators yelled at them to "grow a conscience." A security guard came out and asked the demonstrators to step back from the building, but this seemed to anger the crowd and many got closer to the building and yelled even louder. A large man in an orange-and-brown striped sweater came out of the crowd and started walking toward them. As he got closer, May's first instinct was to run. He was unnaturally tall with a scruffy beard, and he carried a large brown envelope. He walked up the stairs to where they were sitting and handed the envelope to Sid.

"You're late," said the man in a voice that was strangely

high-pitched for someone who looked like such a tough guy.

"The choir was rehearsing at St. Martin-in-the-Fields."

"What were they singing?" asked the man.

"Bach's Magnificat," said Sid.

"How nice," said the man.

"I thought you were coming alone," said the man, looking at May.

"So did I. Do you have the other thing?" asked Sid.

"Yes."

The man took off his backpack and pulled out a rectangular box, which he handed to Sid.

"Be careful with that. Light a match with that baby around and…"

"Thanks," said Sid before the man could finish. "I know it wasn't easy getting this stuff."

"It wasn't as hard as you'd think."

"I have to run. I'll see you tomorrow," said Sid. "Thanks again."

The man shook Sid's hand and nodded to May, then disappeared into the crowd, which was now getting out of hand. May heard the sound of sirens approaching and was sure that the police had been called to deal with the demonstrators. Sid stuffed his packages into a bag he carried on his right shoulder then unexpectedly grabbed May's hand and walked her through a small laneway. She could see that he was heading toward a busy street on the other side. By this point she was feeling really uneasy about being with him, especially after what Chet had told her. She wondered whether the man in the striped sweater was the Diego character that Chet had told her about. When they were halfway through the lane, May stopped and turned to Sid.

"What were those people demonstrating about?"

He turned to face her. His eyes looked wild and he seemed to be lost in thought. His eyes softened for a moment and he said, "They were protesting the company on the fourth floor of that building. They are producing a product that we think is extremely dangerous. They claim that this new product, which is very profitable for them, is safe. But we know it's not."

"Has the government approved it?" she asked. May had learned about how products get approved in her environmental science class. Her teacher had told the class that approval of a product didn't necessarily mean it was safe. It just meant that the risks were not *unacceptable*, a fact that May found highly problematic.

"Yes, it has been approved. But new independent studies show that it is extremely harmful. Rumours are that this company has found a way to cloak certain substances that are banned. These substances are mutagenic. They can change the DNA of a plant, animal, or human. Do you know what that means?"

May looked up at him, speechless. She had finally started to get used to Sid's silence and was thrown off by the long, impassioned soliloquy.

"These can have catastrophic effects on life as we know it," he explained, not waiting for a response. "Many mutagens are carcinogens as well, which are cancer-causing agents," he continued.

May regarded him compassionately, remembering what Chet told her about his cousin's death.

"These substances are not only ruining the planet but they're ruining our health, our very genetic make-up. They are altering us in ways we can't even imagine. These people must be stopped and they need to pay for their destructive behaviour."

May tried to process the speech, not knowing how to respond. Before she could think of anything to say, he took her hand again and started walking. May was perplexed by the fact that Sid had grabbed her hand again and kept staring down at their interlocked fingers.

After several minutes of trying to absorb Sid's sermon, May whispered, "Zorro has told me about some of these substances. He's really paranoid as well about these companies."

Sid turned to her abruptly at the word *paranoid* but said,

"Zorro?" not slowing his pace.

"He's our gardener. He occasionally talks to me about the dangers of the products that are going into our food and into our gardens. He got some award for his environmental gardening practices, so he knows a lot about this stuff. I don't always pay attention because he rants about a lot of things."

Sid slowed down as they came out onto a busy street, where he led her back southwest toward the river. He continued to hold her hand tightly as if he was scared she would get lost like a small child. They walked past the Houses of Parliament, and May stopped for several minutes and just stared in silence, transfixed by the intricate architecture. The place was much larger and more beautiful than she had imagined, and Sid waited patiently for several very long moments while she gazed at it in awe. When May came out of her reverie, one which removed her thoughts from the protest, Sid led her across Westminster Bridge. They made their way toward the London Eye, a large Ferris wheel–type structure that gave visitors a view from over 400 feet above the city in large 10-ton oval, pod-like glass capsules. Sid looked up at the giant structure then looked around as if searching for something. May, feeling suspicious given recent events, said more harshly than she meant, "Who are we meeting here?"

"No one," he said, looking a little hurt. "Chet told me you had a list of things you wanted to see in the city. I thought this might give you a good view."

"Oh...sorry...I..." said May, feeling guilty.

"Don't worry about it. Just wait here," he said, walking away briskly.

May looked at people waiting in a huge line and figured it would take a long time to buy tickets, but Sid was back within a couple minutes, accompanied by a gentleman in a strange suit who shook May's hand and escorted them to an express line. Before she knew it, the three of them stepped into a large pod by themselves. May turned around to see if anyone else was getting in, but the door closed behind them and they slowly started ascending. Zorro's guidebook said that twenty-five people fit into a pod at one time, so she was surprised to have a private one.

"How did you get us on so fast?" asked May. "There's a huge lineup."

"Is there?" said Sid. "I didn't notice."

May would normally have asked for a better explanation, especially given the dubious events enshrouding Sid, but the gentleman who was accompanying them welcomed them, and May realized he was a guide. The guide provided information about how the Eye was built and pointed out landmarks such as Buckingham Palace. May was impressed by the view of the city, but the most impressive thing was the evening sky. The colourful canvas of reds, purples, and pinks cast a magical sparkle over the city. The guide was quiet for the last half of the ride, allowing May to enjoy the view in silence. Sid was quiet as well, barely saying a word for the whole ride. London looked dreamlike and it imprinted itself on May during the ride. As she stepped off the Eye she felt spellbound.

Sid led her back across the bridge, and for the first time in her life she wasn't worried about where she was going or what time she was supposed to be home. She just wanted to stay out and experience as much as possible. Sid never asked whether she wanted to go home or what she wanted to see, he just walked with her. On some level he scared her. At the same time, she acknowledged that without his assertion and confidence, she wouldn't be experiencing any of this.

They walked along the Strand until they reached Somerset House, a beautiful building with over fifty water fountains in its courtyard. The jets were built right into the pavement and alternated between projecting about two feet of water to what looked to May like a twenty-foot spout. She boldly hopped over the jets when they were spouting very low to the ground as Sid watched from beside the fountains with a slight smile. Not wanting to risk getting soaked, May abandoned the fountains and went back out to the street, where they carried on walking and enjoying the warm evening. There was a lushness to London that May hadn't expected, and it made the city seem alive. One would have expected a Caribbean destination to be lush, not an urban setting located on the 51st parallel. But if one looked carefully, greenery peeked through nooks and crannies of the city, defying concrete and brick, and May found the fragrance of the new vegetation invigorating. She felt like she might not ever be able to sleep again. London had somehow bewitched her, and she wanted to stay out all night.

When they came to a busy intersection, she turned to Sid for an indication of which direction they would be walking next, and he said, "I think I'd better get you home. It's getting late."

Again, Sid said very little on the way home, for which May was grateful, because she was in no mood to talk. Polite chatter would seem insignificant at a time like this. Her mother always said that teens weren't capable of true love because they didn't have the maturity to understand such emotions, but May was certain that she had fallen in love, nonetheless. And even though she was in love with a *city* and not a person, it felt real and perfect, the way first love should be.

When they reached Chet's street, Sid walked her up the short path to the front door, and May turned to him with a satisfied smile. She was about to thank him for the tour when he placed his hand on the side of her neck, pulled her toward him and kissed her gently on the lips. She heard the door start to open beside her and pulled away just in time to find Chet standing there.

Looking annoyed and tired, he turned to Sid and said, "Is there something wrong with your phone? I've been a little worried."

"Sorry, mate. I must have turned it off," said Sid.

Sid was already walking back down the front path, leaving May standing there feeling shocked. She pulled herself together quickly as she and Chet quietly walked into the dark house.

"How's Hannah?" May asked to deflect questions from her evening with Sid.

"Badly broken leg and a couple bruises. She was getting her

leg operated on when I left. She'll be in the hospital for a couple days."

"That sounds pretty serious."

"She'll survive," said Chet dryly.

"What time did you get back from the hospital?"

"About an hour ago. Petunia and Auntie Bart were already sleeping, thankfully. So where exactly have you been?" he said, clearly trying to hide how anxious he had been. May suddenly felt extremely guilty for making him worry. There was something about him that reminded her of Gus. Something brotherly.

"We were knocking things off the list. Sid's idea, I swear."

Chet smiled. "Did you have fun?"

"Yes. Listen, I'm sorry we didn't message you," she said. "I have my dad's phone."

"No worries. Maybe you should give me the number, just in case."

At the top of the staircase they wished each other a good night and May walked into her room in a daze then slipped into her pajamas. As she lay down in the small guest bed, she felt her head spinning and let out a sigh. Although she was wired and anxious to relive every moment of the evening, she was asleep as soon as she put her head on her pillow.

CHAPTER 8

May heard Auntie Bart's phone ringing at six-thirty the next morning, then heard a knock on her bedroom door shortly afterwards.

"It's your mother, dear," said Auntie Bart, looking pale-faced and worried.

Auntie Bart scurried out of the room as May put the receiver to her ear.

"Hi Mom."

"Hi May. How are you?"

"I'm okay. Is everything all right?"

"Yes, it's just that I've been trying to call for two days straight and no one has answered. I tried calling you on your father's cell phone as well but with no luck."

"Sorry about that. I haven't turned it on," mumbled May in her semi-conscious state.

"Sorry for calling so early, but I was so worried. I figured it was the only time I could get a hold of you. I don't like to call too late in the evenings because I know Bedrich goes to bed early. Plus, I thought you might be heading out a little early to make sure you got everything done on your list."

Stupid list.

"No, we've been getting up at the regular time," said May.

"Well, I guess I'll let you go back to sleep. We can talk about everything tomorrow night. I'm dying to know how everything is going."

"It's going great. No need to worry. What time are you back tomorrow?"

"I should be back at around seven in the evening."

"Okay. See you then, Mom. Love you."

"Love you too. Bye-bye, dear."

Her mother had sounded a bit concerned, but May thought she had done a good job of hiding the anxiety she felt over the unenviable task of explaining to her mother what had really transpired over the past two days. She slept a couple more hours but her sleep was restless and disturbed. By the time she made her way down to the kitchen for breakfast, Petunia and Auntie Bart had already left to go to the taping of the Penelope Flowerz show. The taping was not scheduled until later in the afternoon, but guests were allowed to watch the crew set up for the show and, according to Auntie Bart, rumour had it Penelope herself might come in early to sign autographs and to chat with members of the audience.

Although May was grateful Petunia had left her alone with Chet, she was shocked by her nanny's behaviour. May wondered what Petunia was planning on telling Reiko. She had never lied to her mother and she certainly wasn't going to back up anything Petunia said that wasn't true. Chet and May hadn't told them anything about the play, and Petunia and her sister had been so preoccupied with their own schedule, they hadn't even asked what May and Chet had been up to.

After a quick breakfast, she joined Chet, who was sitting on the front porch drinking a large cup of steaming tea.

"Good morning, Chet."

"Good morning, *Ophelia*."

"You heard."

"Willow told me this morning. He said you were brilliant. I was just about to wake you up because you are supposed to be at rehearsal in a couple hours."

The reality of the previous day set in at that moment and

May wasn't sure how she felt. The thought of going back on stage with Tucker made her feel ill, but the prospect of not performing no longer seemed an option. As terrifying as it was, it had stirred something within her. Something she had never felt before. Something she couldn't quite put her finger on. But she was terrified nonetheless, a feeling that was amplified by the possibility that Sid might be there watching her rehearse. Sid.

Chet noticed the apprehension on May's face and said, "You really don't need to do this. I can talk to Winterbottom. I'm sure they'll find someone to learn the lines quickly so they can replace you."

"No, of course not," said May, starting to feel like she might throw up.

"I wanted to head out a little early to pick up my trumpet. I forgot it in Hannah's hospital room last night and I have practice with Hammer Dog tonight. Willow said he'd meet us there so he could take you to rehearsal because I have to go straight to the costume shop after the hospital. You're not rehearsing at the Globe Theatre today, and I didn't want you to have to try to find the place yourself."

"It says on the schedule that rehearsals are at a place called Hoxton Hall," said May.

"Yes, it's an old music hall not too far from here," he said. "You'll like it. It's a cool place."

As they walked toward the hospital where Hannah was being cared for, May's thoughts started drifting to the kiss the previous night. Perhaps Sid had mistaken the rapture in her eyes for a fondness for him. She still couldn't process what had happened and wasn't sure what her exact feelings were, but she was incredibly relieved that she had finally been kissed. She had thought about this a lot over the past couple of years. Her friend Charlotte had had her first kiss when she was thirteen and claimed that her younger sister, who was eleven, had already kissed a boy, which May found mildly disturbing. She knew what other girls her age were doing far beyond just kissing and wondered why she was so behind. What if she were eighteen or nineteen when her first kiss came? How awkward would that be? She contemplated why she had never had a boyfriend; She attended an all-girls school and every other moment of her life was strictly scheduled. How was she supposed to find time for a boyfriend or to even kiss someone? Her lips tingled as she thought about Sid's soft lips against hers. Then a queasy uneasiness arose in her stomach. Was this what her friends described as butterflies? She was not sure she liked it.

The hospital was set back from the street and they walked up the long path to the entrance and into lobby, where Willoughby sat reading a magazine with dogs on it.

"It says visiting hours don't begin until two," said Chet.

"I don't think that will be a problem. Hannah's father is on the hospital's board of directors and is a large financial donor to the new hospital wing," said Willoughby.

"How did you know that?"

"We were talking about it at the last mixed social with Hannah's school."

"I don't go to those," said Chet.

"I know. That's why you're behind on all the latest news," said Willoughby, smirking.

The lady at the information desk greeted them courteously and directed them to the fifth floor, where she said Hannah was expecting a visitor.

"Are you two going to wait here in the lobby?" asked Chet.

"And miss a chance to see the human equivalent of sunlight?" replied Willoughby.

"Sarcasm is never the answer, Willow," replied Chet

"We'll come up just in case she decides to take a fancy to you and we have to save you from her loving torture," said Willoughby wryly.

"How nice of you," said Chet, rolling his eyes.

"Actually, I'm just going to run to the gentleman's room for a moment. I'll join you up there," he said. "What room is the joy of the earth in? Or should I just follow the dark cloud of gloom?"

"It's room 512," said Chet, chuckling.

As May turned into the elevator waiting area, she stopped abruptly, causing Chet, who was walking behind her, to bump into her. Sid was standing outside an elevator with a tall blonde girl who wore dark glasses, black high heels, and a trench coat. The girl was fashionably dressed, which was a stark contrast to Sid's torn clothing and safety pins, and they looked strange standing next to one another. Sid's back was toward them and the girl didn't notice Chet and May as she blurted out, "So you're taking care of HRH?"

"Yes," replied Sid.

May and Chet instinctively took a step back, ensuring that Sid did not notice them standing around the corner.

"You need to remember what is important in this life," said the blonde girl.

"I am not going to go back on my word. I'll take care of her on Saturday night."

"And what's going on with the police?"

"They are following my every move," said Sid.

"I don't know why you need to actually be at the Globe on Saturday night."

"I have to be there. Listen I have to go. I'll call you later, okay?" said Sid.

"Oh, I almost forgot," said the blonde, pulling a small box out of her purse. "I picked this up for you."

"Thanks."

The girl handed him the box and kissed him tenderly on the cheek. She walked away and Sid was left standing by himself staring at the small ring-sized box in his hand.

"Hi, Sid," said Chet finally approaching him. "What are you doing here?"

"I was just visiting someone. What are you two doing here?" asked Sid, looking only at Chet.

"I forgot my trumpet in Hannah's room yesterday," replied Chet, suddenly looking embarrassed.

"Well, I'm in a bit of a hurry, so I'll see you this afternoon."

Sid walked off, leaving Chet and May looking at each other

perplexed.

"Weird," said Chet.

Sid hadn't even looked at May, and she felt disappointed. She also felt what must be a pang of jealousy. Her heart was beating fast as she looked down at her old running shoes and thought of the fashionable, fabulous girl Sid had been speaking to. As tattered and disheveled as Sid's clothing looked, May noticed for the first time how beautiful he was and she had to admit that somehow he and this fashionable girl looked like they were in the same league.

"Did you hear what he said about the Globe and the police?" said Chet.

May was still staring at her shoes and didn't respond.

"May?"

"Pardon me?" she said distractedly, looking up at Chet. "Oh, yes," she replied, finally snapping out of the daze. "I wonder what that was all about. What is HRH?"

"Her Royal Highness."

"Of course. The Queen."

"I need to talk to Willoughby," Chet said urgently.

When they reached the fifth floor, they walked down a long corridor that was brightened with sunlight dripping through all the open doors. At the end of the hall was room 512, where the door was slightly ajar. Chet knocked gently and a grumpy voice said, "I told you to just come in!"

He pushed open the door and they saw Hannah sitting up on a bed surrounded by dozens of bouquets of colourful flowers, numerous boxes of half-eaten chocolates and several get well cards. She had a scowl on her face that slackened ever so slightly when she saw Chet and May enter the room.

"Oh, it's just you. I thought you were that annoying nurse," she said with a puckered brow. Then she looked at Chet and said, "Brought your girlfriend?"

Chet looked wounded by the insinuation. "Just here to pick up my trumpet. How are you feeling this morning?"

"How do you think I'm feeling? I'm rotten. I hate this place. The food's awful and…" She hesitated and looked at

May as if something had just dawned upon her.

"Are you the Canadian girl?"

"Yes, I'm May. Nice to meet you." May put out her hand and had to control her urge to curtsy. Hannah just stared at her, leaving May's hand suspended in midair until May gave up her attempt at a handshake and scratched her cheek uncomfortably.

"I heard you are replacing me as Ophelia."

"Just temporarily," replied May.

"That's not what I heard."

May was taken aback, but before she could object, Willoughby sauntered into the room. "Nice flowers. Who died?"

"Did you bring your whole entourage?" said Hannah, glaring at Chet.

Chet ignored her and looked gravely at Willoughby, who had pulled up a chair beside Hannah's bed and was making himself at home.

"What's the matter?" asked Willoughby, noticing Chet's serious stare.

"We need to talk," said Chet. "We just met Sid downstairs with a girl."

"Did he have his dog collar on?" chortled Hannah.

"Not only charming and sweet, but a comedian as well," said Willoughby sarcastically.

"Sid and this girl were having a conversation, which we overheard," said May to Willoughby.

"And this information is interesting because...?" asked Hannah.

Ignoring Hannah's question, Chet turned to Willoughby and whispered, "I think it might have something to do with the activities he's been recently interested in."

"Oh, I see," said Willoughby. "Maybe we should talk outside."

Chet nodded and turned to Hannah. "See you later, Hannah."

"Where are you going?" she replied in a panic. "Why do

you have to go so soon? Don't leave me here while that nurse is on duty. She's really nasty to me…"

"You mean she doesn't see what a pleasant person you can be *down deep*?" said Willoughby in an amused tone. "How she can't see your inner charm is truly a mystery," he added.

"Really funny, Willoughby," said Hannah. "Listen, no one's been here to visit and it would just be nice if there was something interesting to talk about." She looked a little desperate and May thought she saw her eyes water slightly.

"Where are those snotty little friends yours?" asked Willoughby.

"They're really busy," replied Hannah defensively.

Chet looked at Willoughby imploringly. "I can't see how it would hurt, Willow."

"You would trust her?" grimaced Willoughby. Chet and Willoughby were locked in a stare for what seemed like an eternity to May until she decided to break the uncomfortable silence herself.

"I don't think it's a big deal," said May, coming to Chet's rescue. "Do you promise not to tell anyone, Hannah?"

"Oh, please. Do you think any of my friends are interested in what a bloke who wears a dog collar is doing?" she replied in a haughty tone, but subtly gave May a grateful look.

Willoughby shook his head in irritation, then turned to Chet with an inquiring look while he helped himself to a chocolate from the table beside Hannah's bed.

"May and I heard this girl asking Sid if he was going to take care of HRH," said Chet.

"He said he was going to take care of her on Saturday night," added May.

"Did he say what it was exactly that he was going to take care of?" asked Willoughby.

"No," said Chet. "But the girl was asking him about the police."

"He said they were following his every move," said May.

"Considering who he's hanging around with these days, that is definitely strange," said Willoughby.

"Okay, can we back up here?" said Hannah. "What's so strange about that? I used to call my Persian cat HRH."

"It could be nothing, but I'm not sure anymore," said Chet to Willoughby, not acknowledging Hannah questions.

"Actually, there's something else I just thought of," interrupted May. She couldn't believe she had forgotten about the strange encounter with the man in the orange-and-brown striped sweater the previous night. She had been so preoccupied with her mother's impending return and Sid's kiss since she woke up, the rest was a bit of a blur.

"When Sid and I were touring London last night…"

"Sid took you on a tour of London last night?" cut in Willoughby in a jealous tone.

"Yeah, we just walked around the city a bit," she said casually, sensing Willoughby's frustration. "Anyway, Sid met this guy at a protest who gave him a large brown envelope and a box of something. He said to be careful not to light a match around the box."

"I think we should call the police," barked Hannah.

They all turned toward her.

"Wait a minute, Hannah. You can't just call the police on him," said May. For the second time on this trip, she surprised herself with her courage.

"Did I not say we shouldn't have told her?" snarled Willoughby.

Chet put his hand on Willoughby's shoulder. "Let's just calm down for a second. May, which protest were you at?"

"She was at the pro-eco-alliance protest," interjected Hannah before May had a chance to reply. "Why do you think I suggested we call the police?"

The three of them looked at Hannah, perplexed.

"Are we supposed to know what you're talking about?" asked Willoughby.

"Don't you follow the news?" cried Hannah.

Chet, May, and Willoughby looked at each other blankly.

"There was this big protest downtown that was organized by some new radical environmental group," clarified Hannah.

"It turned out violently. There was a big clash with police. You're lucky you didn't get hurt," she said to May in a preachy tone.

"In case you hadn't heard, May," added Willoughby, seeing her inquisitive look, "there have been a growing number of eco-terrorist acts in the last year in London. There have also been a growing number of demonstrations that have been organized around the city, so the police are a little sensitive."

"I don't blame them," said Hannah. "This is no normal group of people. They're like these enviro-radicals. Really extreme. They are being led by some crazy botanist bloke. And now he's recruiting all these people from other groups."

"What exactly is eco-terrorism?" asked May.

"It's sort of a broad term," said Willoughby, "but it usually means someone is doing something, usually illegal or violent, in the name of the environment."

"Do you remember this botanist's name, Hannah?" asked Chet.

"No, but I'll look it up," she said grabbing her tablet and typing onto it frantically. "Diego Taylor is his name. It says here that his group is suspected to have organized the protest but that hasn't been confirmed."

"I can't believe Sid would bring you to a violent demonstration," said Willoughby, sounding incensed.

"It wasn't violent while we were there," said May.

"You must have been there before the police showed up. People were hurt," said Hannah. "It took security and police a long time to get there and by the time they did, things were out of control. The reporter on the news said that police were tipped off that another protest was to take place today at the Penelope Flowerz show. There was all sorts of extra security for the taping today."

May looked at Chet nervously. "Auntie Bart and Petunia are there today watching the show," she said. "Why would they be targeting Penelope Flowerz?"

"The show is sponsored by a product that's made by one of the companies this nutter botanist fellow's group has been protesting against," said Hannah. "I guess he thinks she's sending the wrong message."

"I'm sure they'll be fine, May," said Chet, but she could see he was worried about his grandmother.

"Apparently Penelope Flowerz disapproved of the sponsorship from the beginning," said Hannah. "That's what they said on the *Dish-Now-Britain* show last night."

Hannah looked at May's worried face and added, "If Penelope Flowerz disapproved of the sponsorship, I'm sure the nutter botanist bloke wouldn't target her." Hannah was not great at the sympathetic tone, but May appreciated the sentiment nonetheless.

"Maybe they don't care about whether she approved or not. Maybe they just want to make a point," said Willoughby.

"When you say target," said May, "what exactly do you mean?"

"They burned down a factory a couple months ago and someone was really hurt," said Hannah. "So probably something along those lines."

"I don't think Sid would ever be involved in anything that might hurt innocent civilians," said Chet.

"Are you sure about that?" asked Willoughby.

Chet sighed, remembering asking Sid about this very incident.

"So you think Sid is involved with this eco-crazed terrorist group?" asked Hannah.

Sid and Willoughby looked at her, untrusting.

"Strange that Sid would leave the protest if he was so involved with this group," added Hannah, looking at May.

"May, did Sid say anything about the protest?" asked Chet.

"He said they were protesting a company in the building that produces harmful products. Apparently the company has found a way to cloak dangerous substances which cause cancer."

"I heard that as well," said Hannah. "The company that makes these products has been lying to the public for years. Maybe they really do need to be taught a lesson."

"When did you become such an environmentalist, your dourness?" said Willoughby.

Chet, looking at Hannah inquisitively, said, "Give Hannah some credit. I'm sure she cares about the environment as much as the rest of us."

"Are you my spokesperson now, trumpet boy? I honestly couldn't care less whether all the fish in the ocean drop dead tomorrow. And the only thing that bothers me about the pollution in the air is the fact that is takes the glow out of my otherwise flawless skin. I just think that they shouldn't be selling products that they know are harmful to people."

Willoughby and Chet exchanged annoyed glances.

"So what are we supposed to do now?" asked May.

Hannah sat up straight in her bed, drawing the attention back to herself. "Maybe I can help." She looked keen to relieve herself of the idle confines of her hospital bed.

"How so?" asked Willoughby, looking doubtful.

"My mother has a friend whose son just finished probation for his association with one of these extreme environment groups. Maybe I can find out some information from him. His mother is coming over tomorrow night for champagne tasting night."

"*Champagne* tasting night?" said Chet with a look of disbelief.

"Yes. They're trying a Moët Grand Vintage 2003," she said, ignoring Chet's tone. "It's supposed to be fabulous. Anyway, this hooligan was involved in a fire that was set in a building owned by one of these companies. I'm surprised he just got probation and is not in jail."

"I wonder if he and Sid are in the same group?" asked Chet.

"I don't know. I'll make sure his mother brings him over and I'll see what I can find out. I'll be home by then. Why don't you come by my house on Wednesday morning? I'll even serve breakfast," she added, looking concerned they might decline the invitation. "In the meantime, I'll do some research on my own."

All three of them looked at her.

"You can be useful when you want to be," sniggered Willoughby.

"It's not like there's anything better to do in this godforsaken place," replied Hannah in a proud tone, but May saw a glimmer of excitement her eye.

Chet picked up his trumpet and started heading to the door. "We'd better get going. You two are going to be late for rehearsal," he said, looking at May and Willoughby.

"Are you not going to stay to play trumpet for me today?" asked Hannah.

"I'm not your trumpet boy," replied Chet in an annoyed tone as he exited the room.

"Nice going there, princess," chuckled Willoughby.

"Some people are so sensitive," scoffed Hannah, but May thought she saw a hint of regret on her face as they followed Chet out the door.

CHAPTER 9

Hoxton Hall was a theatre in the East End that May fell in love with immediately. It had a much smaller stage than the Globe Theatre, but the building, which was originally built in 1863, had an inspiring feel, and what it lacked in size, it gained in intimacy and spirit.

May sat with her script on the floor in front of the stage to review her lines, but she was finding it impossible to concentrate with the numerous things plaguing her mind. She was starting to panic about her scene with Tucker, which was scheduled to be rehearsed in fifteen minutes. She was mainly preoccupied, however, by Sid and her confused feelings for him. She wondered about his true character after yesterday's events. To add to her stress, her mother was returning the following evening and would be expecting an account of all the things May was supposed to have done with Petunia over the last couple of days. Even worse, Reiko had a full itinerary for the remainder of the week and May would have to tell her she would be touring London alone, because May was booked into rehearsals.

May muddled her way through the day, trying to deal with Tucker's bad attitude, her constant thoughts about Sid's kiss, incessant worrying about her mother, and the stress of listening to Professor Winterbottom snapping at everyone. She knew Chet was spending a good portion of the day at the costume rental shop making last-minute arrangements for everyone's costumes, including May's. She was three inches shorter than Hannah so her costume had to be altered. Chet returned to pick May up after rehearsal and they stopped on the way home for pizza. Willoughby made plans to meet them the next morning before practice, promising to help May devise a strategy to convince her mother not to ground her for the rest of her life.

Chet told May she seemed preoccupied and asked if she was worried about Petunia and Auntie Bart's safety at the Penelope Flowerz show.

"I'm worried about a lot of things," replied May, thinking it funny that for some reason that was the one worry she had actually forgotten about.

"What are you up to tonight?" she said in an attempt to get her mind off things.

"Hammer Dog booked a great space behind the music shop for practice tonight. I'm going to talk to Sid to see what I can find out. It's about time he and I had a serious talk about what's been going on. If he doesn't want to tell me what he's been up to, I'll have to beat it out of him."

They both laughed.

"By the way, May, I never asked you how your evening was with Sid last night. I mean, besides the fact that he took you to a demonstration with a bunch of radical, violent people."

"And I never asked you how your evening was at the hospital with Hannah, which I'm sure was just as dangerous in its own way," laughed May.

"No real violence with Hannah but pretty close. Just a couple of traumatized nurses and doctors. Good wholesome fun. What about you? Was Sid brooding? He's not like that all the time, you know. Believe it or not, he can actually be quite fun."

May couldn't picture Sid being a jovial slap-on-the-back kind of guy.

"Actually, I couldn't have asked for a nicer night. I saw a few great things and Sid took me on the London Eye. We got our own private pod."

Chet looked at her skeptically. "A private pod on the London Eye?" he said. "That's really unheard of. There are usually huge lineups."

"There *was* a huge lineup, but Sid got us on somehow."

"Leave it to Sid," he said, still looking incredulous. "So what else did you see?"

"We saw the Houses of Parliament. The architecture is so beautiful. I couldn't believe it."

"Did you know that the building is actually officially a palace? It's called the Palace of Westminster. Parts of it have been around for almost a thousand years."

"As much as I enjoyed touring with Sid, I certainly didn't get the same historical context on things without you, Chet."

Chet flashed an appreciative smile.

"I also saw Somerset House," May continued.

"You did all that? Okay, I'm starting to feel guilty for not taking you to more places. I have to make this trip more exciting for you," he said jokingly.

"No kidding." She nudged him and smiled. "You're such a bore."

When they got back to Auntie Bart's house, Chet left to meet Hammer Dog and Sid for practice. May went to her room and turned on her father's cell phone to send Gus a message asking him to call her. The worry she felt about her mother coming home the following night was escalating, and Gus was always a calming force in these situations. A couple minutes later the phone rang and she picked it up quickly.

"Hi, Gus."

"Hey, sis. What's going on?"

"I wasn't sure you'd be home."

"I'm helping Zorro with his Canadian citizenship test this afternoon."

"Is he really going through with it? He always complains about the cold and vows to return to Hawaii. There's no reason for him to stay now that his grandmother has passed away."

"Well, he obviously likes it here more than he lets on. Today we're learning the six responsibilities of Canadian citizenship. Can you guess what they are?" asked Gus.

"Um. Let's see. Shovelling snow? Watching hockey? Being polite? Moose watching? I can't think of any others."

Gus laughed. "Hilarious. Next question for fifty points. What's Canada's national sport?"

"Hockey?"

"Wrong. It's lacrosse."

"Is that on the test?" asked May.

"No, but I was curious to see if you knew the answer. Zorro thought it was curling."

"Not a bad guess."

"So how is your trip going? Did you see everything on the famous list?"

"I don't think you'd believe me if I told you."

"What do you mean? Is everything okay?"

"Sure, everything's fine. How is the hockey tournament going?" May lost her nerve and changed the subject.

"We're undefeated so far. I have a good feeling this year. I'm kind of in the zone."

"That's great," said May distractedly.

"What's going on? I know that tone. It's the one you use when you get one bad grade on your report card and are scared to tell Mom and Dad because you think they're going to be worried you'll turn out like me."

May could feel a lump starting to form in her throat.

"May? Are you there?"

Her normally calm voice took on a tone even she didn't recognize.

"MOM'S COMING BACK TOMORROW NIGHT," she blurted out. "GUS... I'VE BARELY SEEN ANYTHING ON THE LIST AND PETUNIA ABANDONED ME AND I'VE BEEN HANGING OUT WITH PETUNIA'S SISTER'S GRANDSON CHET FOR THREE DAYS AND MOM'S

GOING TO ASK WHY I DIDN'T CALL HER TO TELL HER BUT I DIDN'T WANT TO RAT ON PETUNIA AND MOM IS GOING TO KILL ME." May gasped for breath. "I'M IN BIG TROUBLE."

She was breathing so quickly, she started to wheeze.

"Okay, okay, slow down, May," said Gus, suddenly sounding genuinely concerned. "What have you done for the past three days? You should have called me earlier. What do you mean you're in big trouble? Where has Petunia been and who's this Chet guy?"

"Well that's just the thing. I've spent all my time with him."

There was a short, heavy silence and Gus said frantically, "Oh man, you're not worried you're pregnant, are you?"

"What? GUS! For the love of…! Of course not!" yelled May.

"Thank goodness."

"That's not funny," she exclaimed.

"I wasn't joking."

"It's not like that with Chet. He's just a friend and I can't believe you would think…ugh…never mind."

"Well you said you were in trouble!"

"I meant with mom, Gus. Anyway, Chet's school is putting on a performance of *Hamlet* and I'm going to be playing Ophelia."

"You auditioned for the part of Ophelia in someone's school play?" He sounded half proud, half disbelieving.

"I didn't audition. The girl who was supposed to be playing Ophelia fell off the stage and injured herself, and the role was thrust upon me unsympathetically. I almost hyperventilated on the stage and was mortified because this guy Tucker, whose dad paid off people so he could get the part, is so awful. The performance is on Saturday at the Globe Theatre and there are rehearsals every day and Mom wants to do all these things but I won't be able to do them."

"Okay," said Gus, sounding like he was trying to absorb what she was saying.

"I'm scared Mom isn't going to let me be in the play," said

May.

"That's ridiculous. Of course she will. Do you want to do this play?"

"Of course." She knew she didn't sound sure.

"Mom will let you. I'll call her myself if I have to. Wait a minute; did you say the performance is going to be at the Globe Theatre? You mean that famous theatre you showed me in your guidebook when you were boring me with your itinerary?"

"Yes, and the Queen is going to be there."

There was long silence then Gus burst out laughing. "Okay, okay, I get it. I bugged you too much about the list. You got me. Really funny, May. Hilarious."

"I'm not joking. The bloody Queen is going to be there. Ugh…I can't believe I just said *bloody*. I'm starting to sound like Willoughby!"

"Who's Willoughby?"

"Never mind. What am I supposed to tell Mom? She's going to have a heart attack."

"No kidding. I'm having a heart attack. Who are you and what did Scotland Yard do with my real sister?"

"Thanks, Gus. That's a real help."

Gus let out a compassionate chuckle then said in a soft and serious voice, "Just tell Mom the truth."

"I wasn't expecting that advice from you, Mr. Weasel-my-way-out-of-every-situation."

"I think she'll be proud of you for being in the play."

May let out an unconvinced sigh.

"Okay, I can't guarantee that she won't be mad, but you have to stand up for the things you want. How many times have I told you that?" he said.

"Uh…NEVER??!!"

"Really? Oh well—there's no time to start like the present. And Mom will get over it. She always has with me. And frankly, May, you are sixteen. Don't you find it strange that you are still terrified of Mom?"

"Aren't you?"

"Well yeah, she can be terrifying at times but that has never stopped me from doing things that are important to me that she doesn't agree with. And when she's not furious with me, she is still there for me as a mom. She's still going to love you, no matter what, May. Give her some credit. And it is not like you've actually done anything wrong."

"What about all the things she was looking forward to doing with me?"

"Mom's already been to London several times. Don't worry about her. She can tour around with Petunia. Where *is* Petunia anyway?"

"I haven't a clue. She and Auntie Bart have been busy drinking some sort of weird red drink with fruit in it for most of the trip. They're probably doing that."

They both laughed. May contemplated telling Gus about the situation with Sid but decided it would just worry him. Plus, she didn't want to disclose the details of the kiss. Gus had a list of girls he had kissed in a book he kept on his desk that would intimidate Casanova himself. She was normally able to talk to him about anything, but this was the one subject she felt intimidated about. First of all, he was her brother and it was awkward bringing kissing up. Second of all, the boy she was kissing was a potential terrorist.

May agreed to call Gus the following evening to tell him how things went with Reiko. Shortly after she hung up, she heard Auntie Bart and Petunia come in. They were speaking to Bedrich about their day. She heard them rant and rave about how interesting it was to be there for the filming and how polite and courteous Penelope Flowerz was about signing autographs. They even briefly commented on the amount of security personnel on the set, attributing the heightened security to "potential stalkers."

May went down to the kitchen to chat with them for a few minutes before slipping out to the front porch to wait for Chet. As relieved as she was that they were back safe and sound, she was tired of hearing them carry on about Penelope Flowerz. Neither of them had bothered asking May how her day was or what she had done. She was astounded that they weren't the least bit curious about how she had been spending her time.

Chet's arrival came much earlier than expected. He walked up the front path looking grave, and May jumped up to meet him halfway down the front path.

"Chet, what's wrong?"

"Sid wasn't at Hammer Dog's. He had no idea where he was. And there was an explosion in a new development outside London. There's been a big controversy about this housing development in the news lately because locals think it will destroy some wetlands close by. If the wetlands are destroyed, the plants and animals in the ecosystem will likely be destroyed."

"Was anyone hurt?"

"No. The houses weren't completely built so no one was living in them yet."

"Do you think Sid had something to do with this?" asked May.

"I don't know but it's the same development Sid attended a demonstration for before construction started a few months ago. And I just read that someone from Diego's circle has confirmed that the pro-eco-alliance was responsible."

CHAPTER 10

The next morning, May and Chet met Willoughby at rehearsal a little early. Willoughby seemed concerned about the explosion from the previous day.

"It's been all over the news," said Willoughby. "We really have to do something about Sid. I read more about this group last night and they're pretty scary. Diego looks like a madman. Did you see him?"

"Yes, May and I looked him up again last night."

"May, was he the bloke who Sid gave a package to at the demonstration?" asked Willoughby.

"No, he wasn't the same guy," said May, remembering the man in the orange-and-brown striped sweater.

"If Sid really is involved with this nutter, and he was telling that blonde girl at the hospital that they were going to get something done at the Globe Theatre while the Queen is there …" said Willoughby.

Chet agreed to go by Hammer Dog's house that afternoon to see if Sid had turned up. Then he watched Willoughby and May rehearse before taking May to the costume shop for her final fitting. They arrived back at Hoxton Hall after noon and sat on the floor to watch a few scenes. May noticed that Chet looked on edge and kept fidgeting as if he had to be somewhere, and May had a feeling she knew where that was.

"Chet, is Hannah still in the hospital?"

"Yes. They're releasing her later this afternoon. She is supposed to meet that hooligan bloke at her house tonight."

"Oh, yes. Are you not going to see her?"

"Nope," said Chet, looking defiant yet miserable. "I'm sure she'll live without my trumpet playing for a day."

"Oh, I see," said May, looking at him sympathetically. "You really like her, don't you?"

Chet sighed. "It's so humiliating; I don't even want to talk about it."

May gave him a puzzled look. "You don't have to be embarrassed."

"I *am* embarrassed. She's not what I would normally look for in a girl," he said.

"But she's beautiful."

"So what you're saying is that I should like her because she was born with good looks? Don't you think that's kind of pathetic? Willoughby's right. She's not a nice person."

"I don't think you believe that," said May. "There must be something more that you see in Hannah. She's really not that bad. She's just a little rough around the edges."

Chet looked at her as if she had lost her senses.

"She just needs to soften up a bit," added May.

"Strictly intellectually speaking, she's not what I would aspire to," he said.

"I think she's smarter than you give her credit for. Plus, you can't intellectualize feelings."

"I'd like to think I can. And even if I overlook that, I would like to think that the girl I admire is someone who is kind and considerate and thoughtful."

"You're being too analytical."

"This is coming from a girl whose family books their meals one month in advance."

"How did you know that? Ugh! Never mind. Just get out of here. Go see her." May handed him his sweater and pushed him toward the door. "I know how to get home by myself now," she added.

"I'm going to get an earful from Willow about this one," said Chet as he reached the door.

"Don't worry about Willoughby," said May. "Just make sure you're back before seven, because that's when my mom is getting home and I need all the help I can get."

"What are you going to say to her?" asked Chet.

"I have absolutely no idea."

Willoughby, who had been in a smaller rehearsal room, found May on the floor and sat next to her. He asked May where Chet had gone and grumbled incessantly when he found out his friend was visiting Hannah.

"I told him to stop going to see her. She only tolerates him because he caters to her every whim. It's bloody pitiful."

"Willoughby, is it possible you're overreacting a bit? After all, she's trying to help us figure out what Sid's been up to. She's been doing research."

Willoughby looked at May as if she were crazy. "He brought her soup the other day. You wouldn't catch me bringing someone soup like some sort of servant."

"She's not *that* bad."

"How could you say that after meeting her? I thought you were a sensible girl."

Willoughby shook his head in disgust and started reading an equestrian magazine with a scowl on his face. When he calmed down, he taught May techniques on how to get into character and block out the fact that there was an audience watching her. Unfortunately, there was no technique to help May to block out the fact that one of the audience members would be the Queen.

As they started wrapping up before May's final scene, Willoughby approached her awkwardly. "What are you doing after rehearsal, May? I thought you might want to go visit a couple things around the city. Then maybe we could grab a bite to eat?"

"That's really nice of you, Willoughby, but I need to get back to Auntie Bart's right after practice because my mother is coming back tonight. Maybe we can do something tomorrow. That is, if I'm not grounded for the rest of my teenage years."

"I forgot about your mother. But the afternoon is still young," he pressed. "I'm sure there's still plenty of time to see a couple of things."

"I really want to head back to Chet's. Why don't we try tomorrow after rehearsal?" said May.

"Okay," said Willoughby, sounding disappointed. "I know this great little Indian place."

"That sounds fun. I love Indian food."

Willoughby left and May finished her last scene feeling positive and more confident. Professor Winterbottom seemed pleased with her performance, judging by the lack of yelling May had to endure.

When rehearsal ended, May chatted with some of the other cast members and then started packing up to head home to meet her mother. She was putting her script and her sweater into her bag when she felt a hand on her shoulder. Startled, she turned quickly and found Sid standing there.

"It makes me nervous to think that there's a list out there with stuff not crossed off it," he said in a disturbingly soft and gentle voice. His face was kind and bright and furnished with a slightly roguish grin. He was dressed in jeans and wore a light blue button-down shirt. His hair was unspiked and hung down just above his chin.

"Sid, I can't go anywhere tonight. My mother's coming back."

"At what time?"

"At around seven."

"Plenty of time."

"Plenty of time for what?" asked May.

But Sid was already walking swiftly out of the hall. May ran to catch up with him and as they reached the exit said, "Sid, you don't understand..."

But he kept walking so fast, May had to jog to keep up with him, and she got to the Tube station slightly out of breath. She was going to protest when he smiled at her and said in his disarmingly quiet and tender voice, "Come on. It will be fun. I'll get you home on time, I promise."

The Tube ride took forever and May had no idea where she was going. One thing she knew was that she was going west and Chet's house was in the opposite direction. Sid kept saying, "Just a couple more stops," whenever May looked like she was about to panic. She wanted to ask him about the protest and what he had been discussing with the girl at the hospital but she somehow couldn't bring it up. When she was with Sid, asking him if he was involved in a radical group that might be plotting something illegal seemed ridiculous, because he appeared so incapable of such things.

"Are we almost there?"

"Just a couple more minutes," he said, smiling broadly at her.

Why was he being so nice to her and showing her around the city? And why was he in such a good mood with his cute grin? She was scared to even think about it. She was so mad at herself for trusting him. She had read countless books and seen countless movies where the girl trusts someone she barely knows, and it's so obvious to everyone that the guy is bad news and possibly a psychopathic killer or a terrorist, but the girl is too stupid to notice.

"London's got such brilliant parks, I thought you might want to see a couple of them," Sid finally revealed as he led her off the Tube at St. James's Park. May didn't remember St. James's Park being on her list, but as if reading her mind again, Sid said, "It's on the way to Hyde Park."

Hyde Park was definitely on her list. Sid reached for May's hand as he started toward the park. Despite what she originally perceived as an overconfident gesture, his assertion didn't seem brash or arrogant to her now. It felt sincere, kind, and gentlemanly at that moment and the touch of his hand took her breath away.

It was a sunny and warm afternoon. Kids were playing and the flowers were in bloom. Sid told her about the different trees and plants in the park, his voice thoughtful and expressive. On the other side of St. James's Park was Hyde Park, which was several times the former's size. Again, they passed beautiful gardens and Sid pointed out all the different types of plants. She was impressed by his knowledge of flowers, shrubs, and trees, many which he explained didn't grow in parts of Canada. In the middle of Hyde Park was a long pond filled with ducks and swans.

It felt like they had been walking for an hour, and as they reached the end of the pond, clouds were covering the sun and a cool wind was picking up. A few minutes later, gusts of winds were blowing intensely and it started raining sideways. Sid and May ducked behind a large tree and May fumbled for the compact umbrella Zorro had insisted she bring. They huddled under the umbrella, which beat against the back of their heads due to the intense wind. They stood there for several minutes before May started to feel the rain penetrate her shoes and her jeans. Sid put his arms around her and she closed her eyes and buried her face in his chest as the noise of the flapping umbrella beat in her ears. Being in Sid's arms was almost disorienting. She could feel his heart beating against her cheek as he pulled her in closely.

She was surprised when the wind died down just a few minutes later. The rain had stopped as suddenly as it had started.

"I can't believe how fast the weather changes here," said May.

"Welcome to London."

They were able to continue along the wet path on until they reached the end of the park and a beautiful red brick building sitting in front of extraordinary gardens.

"This is Kensington Palace," said Sid. "It's where Princess Diana lived."

"It's beautiful," replied May, a slight shiver in her voice.

Her jeans were soaked and she felt the dampness in her bones.

"I'm taking you somewhere you can have a warm tea," said Sid, leading her to a smaller red brick building beside the palace that housed the café Chet had spoken about called the Orangery. At the entrance of the café was a table of beautifully displayed fruits and cakes. A pile of scones was heaped in a large tower that threatened to topple over. The décor was sparkling white and the large bright windows that ran from the floor to the ceiling looked out on the gardens. The waitress came and Sid ordered sandwiches, tea, and cake for the both of them. As they awaited their order, May noticed how conservatively Sid was dressed. No studs. No boots. No safety pins. As she looked around at everyone in the place, thinking Sid almost fit in, her eye caught a tall blond man who was sitting against the window. He had a large scar on his face that ran from the middle of his cheek to the bottom of his chin and she noticed he had looked up at them discreetly several times. He wore a creased white shirt that was stained with what looked like coffee or some other dark liquid, and he had scruffy facial hair that grew in uneven patches, making his beard look like straw.

Her suspicions about Sid suddenly came back and she wondered what she was doing here. Maybe Sid was just using her to look like he fit in so he could conduct his business. No one would suspect any illegal activity in a place like this. The waitress came with their order and May spilled her tea while scanning the room for other dubious-looking characters.

"Are you looking for someone, May?" asked Sid, noticing her strange behaviour.

"Um. No. Why do you ask?"

He looked puzzled. "Do you not like the place?" he asked in a slightly disappointed voice. "It's not really my type of place, but I thought you would like it."

"I do like it. It's so nice. It's—more than nice. It's—fantastic. Thank you for taking me here," she stuttered. "I like the way they cut the crusts off the sandwiches," said May as she looked at her plate.

"Welcome to England," he laughed.

May had never seen Sid laugh before and was taken aback at how stunning he was with his flawless teeth and bright blue eyes. She remembered her words to Chet about feelings not being intellectual. Gus had always told her to trust her instincts but she was not sure this was sound advice. One minute she trusted Sid, the next minute she thought he might be meeting a shady person behind a bush to acquire a questionable package.

While all this was going on in her head, Sid reached across the table without warning and kissed her. Despite the many questions in her mind surrounding him at the moment, she was physically incapable of not reciprocating. As he felt her respond to him, he kissed her harder. After the kiss, which was so staggering that she would have thought it inconceivable five minutes beforehand, she looked down at her sandwiches awkwardly and said, "I'm just going to finish these now."

Sid laughed at her and said, "You do that, May."

When May finished her last sandwich, Sid insisted on paying the bill. They exited Hyde Park at the north end and walked through a beautiful residential area. She looked back as they walked away from the café to make sure the man with the scar wasn't following them, but he was nowhere in sight.

May didn't bother asking where they were going this time and allowed herself to be intrigued but the unknown, a concept previously foreign to her. They arrived at a pedestrian tunnel about ten minutes later, and when they walked through it, they came out in a pretty area that overlooked a canal. There were barges and boats in the water, and Sid led her to a small open-air boat that some people were boarding. Sid paid for the tickets and they stepped onboard, where they sat on a wooden bench on the port side.

"We're going to take the canal through Regent's Park up to Camden Lock."

"Is that where the Camden Market is?"

"That's the one. Most shops will be closed by the time we get there, but your mother is coming home soon, so we won't be able to stay long anyway."

Her mother. May had lost track of time again, just as she had done the last time she was with Sid. She was a little alarmed at this power he had over her to lose track of all scheduling. She wasn't used to this freedom and wasn't sure whether she liked it. Now she was stuck on a boat with no way off.

"Sid, how long is the trip?"

"It's only forty-five minutes."

Only forty-five minutes? she thought, exasperated. But her frustration dissipated quickly as she viewed the beautiful scenery of the canal, which was lined with fragrant flowers and trees as well as cute boathouses painted in lively colours, the London Zoo, and an aviary filled with chattering birds. Sid continued to point out the names of plants and flowers as he had done earlier in the parks, and as May listened to him, she thought of how Hannah had mentioned that Diego was a botanist when they were visiting her in the hospital. Sid seemed to know a lot about the flora of the city, and May figured he would have a lot in common with Diego. When they disembarked and walked through the crowded streets along Camden Market to the Tube station, May got up the courage to ask him the question that had been burning inside her.

"Sid, did you know that the demonstration we were at the other day turned violent?"

"I heard," replied Sid, continuing his brisk pace and not looking up.

"People were hurt."

He glanced over at her quickly. "You were never in danger."

"How do you know that unless you were involved?"

"Why would you think I had anything to do with it?"

"Are you denying you knew about it in advance?"

"I'm not denying anything. I'm just curious to know why you think I had anything to do with it."

He had finally slowed and his eyes became slightly accusing. May's voice started to tremble. "You knew what the demonstrators were protesting about and referred to them as 'we' as if you were part of the group."

Sid's face softened a bit and he said, "Yes, I knew there was going to be a protest."

"Plus, you and this Diego guy both like botany and seem to have a lot in common."

Sid turned to look at her with a burning stare. "How did you know I knew Diego? Did Chet put you up to asking me all these questions? Is that why you're here?" he said angrily.

"No, of course not, Sid. You're the one who asked me to come here with you." May knew she had blundered and tried to recover to no avail. "You knew all the names of the trees and plants in St. James's Park and Diego is a botanist. I just figured..."

Sid shot her a look that was half hurt, half livid. He was quiet the rest of trip and May felt horrible. She fought to control a lump in her throat that threatened to turn into tears. They walked up Auntie Bart's front path where Chet was on the porch waiting for May with the same worried look on his face he had the last time she was out with Sid.

"I brought your little informer back safe and sound," said Sid coldly.

"What are you talking about?" Chet sounded annoyed.

"I don't need to answer to you or anyone else about where I am, what I'm doing and who I associate with. And the next time you want to find out information about me, why don't you just grow a backbone and ask me yourself instead of sending your little snitch here to find out information."

"Watch your mouth. Don't talk about her like that."

But Sid was briskly walking back along the path toward the street.

May stood in shock with tears in her eyes. Chet put his arm around her and led her inside.

"Come on. Your mum will be home soon. I'll deal with him later."

They went upstairs to Chet's bedroom with a pot of tea and sat on his bed.

Chet was strangely calm after Sid's outburst, and his composure settled May, who was still shaking but no longer felt like crying.

"Where are Petunia and Auntie Bart?" she asked.

"They're skulking around the backyard like a couple of fugitives. Petunia looks a little worried. I reckon she's trying to think up an excuse for deserting you these past four days."

Chet looked at May inquisitively and checked the tea to see if it was brewed. "So what exactly were you doing with Sid?"

"He came by and asked if I wanted to see some things on my list," said May apologetically.

"I guess that's why he wasn't home when I went by his house this afternoon."

"Sorry, Chet. I should have sent you a note." May felt guilty and tears welled up in her eyes again.

"No worries," said Chet. He looked at her contemplatively then said, "Funny, the first time Sid took you out, I thought he was just doing me a favour, but obviously there's more to it than that. I mean, I have never seen him wearing a blue button-down shirt. It is not exactly his style. If I didn't know any better, I might think he was trying to impress you."

May blushed deeply. Chet wore a strange look that she couldn't quite read.

"So where did he take you?" he asked curiously.

"We walked through St. James's Park and Hyde Park and saw Kensington Palace. We went to the Orangery for tea then he took me on a boat ride to Camden Market."

"So he took you to Little Venice," said Chet.

"Is that what that pretty area was called where the boat ride started?"

"Yes. The poet Robert Browning used to live in the area. It reminded him of the waterways of Venice. I don't suppose that was on your list?"

"No," said May, finally allowing herself to smile. "I'm seriously throwing the list in the garbage."

"Thatta girl," said Chet, making May laugh. "So what did you say to make him so mad?"

"I asked him about whether he had known about the protest, which he didn't deny. Then I kind of mentioned Diego. He got really angry and wanted to know if you had put me up to asking him that question."

Chet let out a sigh and poured May a cup of tea. They both sat for a few minutes until in his customary fashion of lightening the tone, Chet said, "Did you know that Kensington Palace isn't officially in Hyde Park? It's in Kensington Gardens, which is actually a separate park."

May laughed. "What would I do without you, Chet?"

She put some milk and sugar in her tea. Outside Chet's bedroom, they heard a car pull up to the curb. Chet walked to the window and looked out.

"Your mother's here."

CHAPTER 11

As they walked down the stairs, Chet grabbed May's arm and said, "We never really talked about what you were going to say to your mum about the play and everything else."

May paused for a moment to think about the situation. She looked up at Chet and sighed, unsure. "I think I'm just going to tell her the truth."

"I'm sure she'll understand," said Chet, looking unconvinced. Then he added, "Maybe I can talk to her."

May smiled at him. She felt so indebted to him for everything he'd done so far, from saving her vacation to being a friend, even though they barely knew each other. And now he was willing to talk to her mother. She couldn't imagine what he would say but was convinced he'd assume some sort of blame if he thought it would get May out of trouble.

She reached out, grabbed his hands and said, "Thanks for the offer, Chet, but I think I'm on my own here." Then she scurried downstairs to the door nervously while Chet went to the backyard to let Auntie Bart and Petunia know that Reiko had arrived. May's mother piled into the kitchen with her bags, hugging May and maneuvering herself around the small area.

"I'm so sorry I'm late. The traffic was awful."

Petunia and Auntie Bart came into the kitchen and greeted

Reiko with hugs though they still had sheepish looks on their faces.

"Welcome back. Have you eaten, Reiko?" asked Auntie Bart.

"Yes, I ate earlier. I'm not hungry."

"Well, I'll put on the tea then," said Auntie Bart, opening the china cabinet and removing an antique-looking teapot with blue flowers on it. May sat beside her mom as Petunia unwrapped some pound cake that had been left on the table.

"How has everything been, May?"

"I've had such a good time," she replied, putting off the inevitable. "What about you, Mom? How was your work? Was there anything interesting to do there?"

Reiko told May about the receptions, lectures and a golf tournament at the conference. As they finished their tea and cake, Reiko turned the subject to May's time in London again.

"Well, we haven't got everything on the list done, but I've still had an incredibly *interesting* time," said May.

Petunia and Auntie Bart exchanged uncomfortable glances.

"Interesting time?" said Reiko, sensing, as mothers often do, that something was afoot.

May gave Reiko an apologetic look and said, "I haven't missed much, Mom. I missed a few things but saw a bunch of things I hadn't planned on seeing and did a lot of things I didn't plan on doing. It turned out pretty good. I went to St Martin-in-the-Fields. There was a choir singing Bach's Magnificat and it was just beautiful."

Petunia shifted in her seat and asked Auntie Bart to bring her an after dinner drink.

"What would you like, Petunia?" asked Auntie Bart.

"Anything!" replied Petunia urgently.

Noticing the nervous look on Petunia's face, May was suddenly struck by a wickedly mischievous feeling, a sensation that arose in her for the first time in her life. She continued with her account of the events of the past few days, but her tone had changed from apologetic to empowered.

"I also went to this lovely tea room in Soho. There was

really cool art on the wall and the sandwiches were out of this world. The English really do tea and sandwiches well. I think afternoon tea is a good tradition. I enjoyed it so much, I went to the Orangery at Kensington Palace and had the most delicious sandwiches there as well. Don't you think the sandwiches are delicious at the Orangery, Petunia?"

Petunia, whose bewildered face had turned a dark shade of red, smiled through gritted teeth at Reiko and replied, "Yes, sandwiches are always very good at the Orangery."

Reiko was looking baffled by May's description of the events and seemed curious about the dynamic between May and Petunia.

"Chet was nice enough to take me to couple places while Petunia and Auntie Bart went to the Penelope Flowerz show."

"Oh, I see," said Reiko, who looked questioningly at Petunia then turned her glance back to May.

"I meant to tell you that on the phone yesterday, but it was early so it slipped my mind," said May.

May saw her mother's eyebrows raise. She knew accountants never let things *slip their minds,* and that sort of comment drove Reiko nuts.

"I was fine, Mom. Chet's been a great host. He's really..." May was trying to think of an adjective that would push Petunia's buttons. "... responsible."

Reiko looked like she didn't know whether to be pleased or furious, but her face lit up somewhat, and she said, "Well, it was nice that you had someone your own age to hang around with. Chet seems like a really good, polite boy. It was nice of him to show you around."

Petunia had abandoned her drink and got up to start putting dishes away. May's mother glanced at Auntie Bart courteously, though she still had a confused and somewhat displeased look on her face.

"Mom, why don't we go put your bags upstairs," said May, needing some time to regroup. She helped her mother deposit her suitcases in the guest bedroom, and Reiko started to put her clothes in the little bureau beside the bed she would be sleeping in for the next few days.

"So tell me what you missed on the list, and we might be able to fit it into our schedule in the next couple days."

"Mom, you can't even fit an unscheduled bathroom break into that schedule," replied May with a sardonic smile, amused at herself for using Gus's line. She was still not sure how she was going to tell her mother that she was supposed to be rehearsing at Hoxton Hall at nine a.m. the following morning. She thought she might be able to appease her mother by meeting her after rehearsals and spending the afternoon with her, but she wasn't sure how she was going to get out of going to Windsor Castle on Thursday. They had watched videos about the castle right before the trip, and May knew her mother was looking forward to visiting it. May took a deep breath, closed her eyes and in as natural a voice as she could muster, blurted, "Mom, I actually have other plans for the rest of the week."

Reiko paused for a moment and stared at May as if she'd misheard. "Other plans? May, what are you talking about?"

May took a deep breath then launched into an account of the events of the past few days, trying to sound as nonchalant and natural as possible. She figured if the story was delivered in a calm manner, her mother might take it better, a method she'd seen Gus use on numerous occasions. May limited her account to the events of the play and made it seem that the things she had done with Sid were actually done with Chet. She thought it might take a while for her mother to absorb the fact that she had been gallivanting around a strange city for four days with one teenaged boy, let alone another.

She was diplomatic in her treatment of Petunia, saying she thought she might have been unwell from the jetlag the first couple of days.

"After that, most of the time was spent at rehearsals, so there was no point in Petunia being there. So, since I'm in the play now, I have to be at rehearsals for the rest of the week," she concluded, as if she were telling her mother about the weather. "I hope that's okay."

Reiko listened to her in total silence with a blank expression. As May recounted the events of the past few days, she thought they didn't sound as bad as half the things Gus had done over the years, but by the time she finished, her mother wore a look that May had never seen before, even when Gus had done something really bad. She found it alarming but she waited patiently for her mother's response. Judging from the scary contortion appearing on Reiko's face, it was apparently too much for her to process. The shock seemed to render her temporarily mute. May had never disobeyed her mother, finished her homework one minute late, or snuck out of her bedroom window late at night like her brother. She thought she might deserve a little leeway, even though in the past three days she had been wandering around one of the biggest cities in Europe without adult supervision. When her mother didn't respond, she said, "Mom, they've sold tickets for the play. All the proceeds are going to charity. There are going to be some distinguished guests there and it's at the Globe Theatre. Have you heard of the Globe Theatre? Mom? Are you listening? There are going to be some important people there."

Her mom, looking slightly like a lunatic blurted out, "I don't care if the Queen of England is going to be there!!!"

May had never heard her mother's voice raised like that, and for a moment she stood frozen. "Actually, Mom, I think the Queen *will* be there," she said in a whisper.

But the comment didn't register. May guessed the prospect of having two kids like Gus was not a happy one for Reiko. After a couple of uncomfortable minutes, May's mother's expression grew determined and resolute, and May now recognized what she and Gus called "the twenty and three quarters look." This meant Reiko was going to launch into a series of questions she didn't necessarily want answers to. May had heard the tirade before on occasions where Gus had been caught doing something really bad, and she braced herself.

"So what you're trying to tell me is that you've been going to rehearsals for a play for the past few days instead of visiting the city with Petunia and Auntie Bart?"

One down. Nineteen to go.

"Why didn't you tell me on the phone?"

Question two.

"Why didn't you call me to tell me that Petunia had relinquished her duty as a responsible adult? Where was Petunia? Were you alone in the city at any time? Do you realize what could have happened to you?"

Three, four, five, six. This might be worse than she thought.

May cut in before her mom could continue. "Mom, I'm sixteen."

"In a strange city with a boy you barely know! Did he try anything funny with you? I'm not naïve, you know. I know what sixteen-year-olds are doing these days. I knew I should have had that talk to you about condoms, but your father was dead against it. The condoms should be latex, you know. I learned that at the 'parenting teens' seminar at your school."

"What? I don't need bloody condoms, Mom." There she went with the *bloody* again. "What is wrong with everyone?" said May, infuriated. "Chet is only a friend and I learned about condoms in grade three."

Reiko, ignoring May's retort, looked undeterred. "And why is it that …? I mean, do you think it's appropriate to…? When I was a young girl I would have never dared….! I mean, how is it that this generation…?

And there they were. The three quarters of a question, questions.

"And was that other boy there? The one with the crazy hair and tattoos?"

May froze, her breathe stopping for a quick instant, bewildered by her mother's reference to Sid. Reiko had struck a nerve and May could only stare blankly. She knew her mother would notice the change in her behaviour. Should she tell the truth? She'd not only have to endure another twenty questions about Sid, which she was in no mood to answer, but she would be in *really* big trouble now. Petunia would probably get fired for that one. She heard Gus's voice telling her to just tell her mom the truth. She hadn't actually done anything that bad. It was only a kiss, and it was pretty innocent compared to what other girls were doing. Did she just say *innocent*? Either way, it was none of anyone's business.

Her mom was staring at her furiously, waiting for an answer. May felt defeated. She wasn't ready to tell her mother about Sid. That was private. Tears started to well up when she heard her mother say, "What did you say about the Queen?"

May looked up at Reiko, momentarily confused. "What?"

"The Queen. You said something about the Queen."

The expression on Reiko's face had turned from frantic to slightly inquisitive.

"Oh. That. Yeah—she's going to be at the play."

"And you're going to be in this play?

"Yes."

"In front of the Queen?"

"Yes."

"Are you talking about the Queen of England?"

"Yes, Mom. We are in England right at the moment, so I think you could just call her the Queen."

May was surprised at her sarcastic tone. Her mother always said that sarcasm was the lowest form of human interaction.

Reiko sat there for a few long minutes. There were too many emotions on her face to read and she began to look a little scary. It was as if she desperately wanted to continue to be furious but that last piece of information made it physically and emotionally impossible. Reiko suddenly stood up, folded her arms and started pacing back and forth like a mad scientist. She continued this for a couple moments then stopped suddenly and said, "I'd like to have a word with Petunia. Please excuse me."

She walked out the door and down the stairs. May waited a couple of moments then crept down the stairs after her. She was curious to see what Petunia was going to say to defend herself, but she found her mother in an empty kitchen.

When Reiko realized that Petunia and Auntie Bart had managed to slip out of the house, she turned her attention back to May.

"What about the day trip we planned to Windsor Castle on Thursday? We talked about it so much," she said in a voice that now sounded tired and disoriented.

"Maybe I can go to rehearsal on Thursday and you can go with Auntie Bart and Petunia. I have rehearsal all that day and it's two days before the play."

"You most certainly will not stay behind! I have already purchased tickets. We are going to Windsor Castle for the day and I am not leaving you alone in a strange city with a sixteen-year-old boy who…"

"He's seventeen and his name is Chester, Mom. And a few minutes ago you were saying how happy you were that I found someone my own age."

May was waiting for her mother to mention Sid again, but to her relief, she just said, "I need to be alone for a few minutes, May, if you'll just excuse me." She walked out the front door and sat on the front porch. May stood frozen at the kitchen table for a long time before making her way upstairs, where she knocked on Chet's bedroom door, wondering if he was home. He didn't answer, so she went back to her room, where she sat dejectedly on the bed. She contemplated what she would do if her mother refused to let her be in the play. Her mother wasn't a big proponent of the arts. She didn't understand its value. Reiko always said that if math wasn't involved in an activity, it wasn't worthwhile. May was very different than her mother in that way.

The thought of Professor Winterbottom's reaction to her mother's potential refusal kind of scared her, but what she was most scared of was how she herself would react. She knew she would be crushed. She considered ways she could still be in the play if her mother refused. Perhaps she could pretend she was sick and then sneak out to go to the Globe on Saturday night. When she visualized herself climbing out the window, she giggled. For the first time in her life she really understood why Gus snuck out of the house at night.

As her thoughts wandered to the various scenarios of what might happen, she thought she heard voices downstairs. She crept down the stairs and to her surprise found Chet, Willoughby and a younger boy talking to her mother at the kitchen table. They all looked up at her as she walked in, and the younger boy stood up and rushed over to her with his hand outstretched.

"You must be May. I'm Hamish McGregor, Willoughby's brother."

"Nice to meet you, Hamish," said May as she put her hand out to meet his. But instead of shaking May's hand, Hamish took it and kissed it. May looked at him incredulously and tried to suppress her amusement. She turned to Chet and Willoughby with a questioning look and Willoughby said, "We just came here to tell your mother about your brilliant acting skills."

"Willoughby was telling me what a difficult part it is and how you perform so well," said May's mother with a look of pride.

May looked at Willoughby affectionately, and he winked at her.

"May, I will allow you to be in the play and go to rehearsals, but we are going to Windsor Castle on Thursday," said Reiko, firmly but kindly.

May accepted that fact that she would have to balance Winterbottom and her mom. There had to be some sort of compromise.

Chet said, "We'll talk to Winterbottom. I'm sure she'll agree."

"She doesn't have much of a choice. Who else can play that role?" added Willoughby.

"I'm sure you wouldn't want to let down the Queen of England," said Reiko somewhat gushingly.

"Thanks, Mom," said May, walking over to hug her.

"You three boys are welcome to come to Windsor Castle with us if you like."

"There's no way I'll be able to miss rehearsal," said Willoughby, "but thanks for the offer."

"I would be delighted to accompany you, Mrs. Abbott,"

said Hamish.

"Hamish, I'm supposed to be babysitting you on Thursday. Mum asked me to take you to rehearsal with me," said Willoughby.

"I do not need to be babysat by someone who has a lower IQ than I," replied Hamish proudly. "Mrs. Abbott has invited me, and I have no intention of refusing her gracious invitation."

Willoughby looked at his younger brother and let out a deep, annoyed sigh. "We'll talk to mum."

They chatted for a few more minutes then Willoughby said they had to get Hamish home.

"I'm sorry to cut this visit short, Mrs. Abbott," said Hamish as they made their way to the front door. "I look forward to the opportunity to talk to you some more about your admirable profession. I am contemplating future career plans for myself and would be thrilled to hear first-hand the exciting day-to-day life of an accountant. I mean, what would we do without accountants? We'd all be paying too much tax, that's what. I mean, I don't pay tax myself, but it's something that irks me constantly. Some nights, I can't even sleep thinking about it."

Reiko stifled a laugh and said, "We can talk about it some more if you're able to come along on Thursday."

While Hamish made arrangements for Reiko to call his mother, Willoughby whispered under his breath to May and Chet, "Sorry, I had to bring the little twit along. He may have an IQ of 165 but that doesn't make him less of an idiot."

"Is he visiting from Scotland?" asked May.

"Yes, both he and my mum are in town to see the play. My mother decided to come into London a couple of days early to visit some old school friends. She had plans with a friend tonight and asked me to babysit."

"Does he always talk like that?" asked May.

"Yeah, he's a sixty-five-year-old trapped in a twelve-year-old body. He's a real freak."

May thanked Willoughby and Hamish for coming and then

headed off to bed early.

May's mother said she wasn't tired and was going to stay up for a while. She usually went to bed extremely early, so May guessed that she was staying up to wait for Petunia, who still had not come out of her hiding place. May couldn't imagine where she had gone but was glad that she had settled everything with her mother. She went to bed and slept soundly.

*   *   *

Hannah messaged Chet early the next morning to say she was back in the hospital to check for a potential infection so they would have to postpone their meeting. She'd met with the 'hooligan' the previous evening but preferred to discuss their conversation in person. Chet decided to spend the day in the library to study for upcoming exams and agreed to meet May and Willoughby after their dinner.

At rehearsal, May had the unfortunate task of telling Professor Winterbottom that she would be unable to attend the following day. As soon as the words were out of May's mouth, the professor's hair started sprouting wings. May promised to practice her lines during the drive to Windsor, but Winterbottom was still not pleased and she threatened to find another Ophelia. May told her that if she could find an Ophelia to replace her, that was understandable. Gus had taught her that a good poker face was one's best ally in situations like these. She thought she must have learned a pretty good one after watching him all these years because Winterbottom finally relented and offered to hold a rehearsal at her own house the following night to make up for the lost time.

To May's surprise, Tucker, who she never spoke to aside from when they were on stage together, agreed to meet them as well. Several students had told May and Tucker that there was great chemistry and tension between them, and although May was appalled that she might have any sort of connection with Tucker, she had to admit she worked well with him.

Rehearsals went especially smoothly that day. Willoughby

mentioned their dinner plans at the Indian restaurant several times and looked distracted and nervous the whole day. When rehearsal was finally over Willoughby approached her awkwardly.

"I'm just going to get my things in the small rehearsal room, then we can go."

"Okay, take your time," she said gathering her own things and putting them into her bag. A few minutes later she felt a hand on her shoulder. She knew it was Willoughby but she still felt butterflies in her stomach hoping she'd see Sid when she turned around. Instead, she was greeted by a tall brown-haired woman wearing dark sunglasses who pulled out a badge.

"Ms. Abbott, I'm special agent Darwin Lee of the Security Service. I'd like to have a word with you at headquarters. My car's just outside."

"I don't understand. What's the Security Service?"

"MI5. The British Intelligence Agency. I investigate threats to national security such as terrorism and the like."

"What is this about?"

"We can discuss this down at headquarters. This is not a good place to talk, Ms. Abbott."

"You can't expect me to go with a complete stranger," said May suspiciously, wondering whether she would be kidnapped.

"I'm not going to kidnap you," said Darwin rolling her eyes.

"How did you know I was thinking that?"

"I can tell by your body language. It's my specialty. Sixteen-year old's watch too many crime shows."

"What if I refuse to come with you?"

"Well technically, being a foreign national and a minor, I don't have the authority right at the moment to *make* you come with me. Heck of a lot of paperwork. So I'm asking you politely. If you don't come however, it will ultimately make things more difficult for you. And given your mother's strict, conservative nature, I'm quite certain she won't be amused if I pay her a visit to show her this."

Darwin pulled out a photo from her purse and handed it to

May. It was a picture of May kissing Sid in front of Auntie Bart's house.

"Romantic isn't it, young love?" said Darwin sarcastically.

May was too shocked to respond and followed Darwin robotically to the door where she heard Willoughby calling her name.

May and Darwin turned around as he was catching up to them.

"May, where are you going?"

"I have to go to the British security service place."

"MI5? Is this because of Sid?"

Darwin showed Willoughby her badge and grabbed a bouquet of flowers that he had in his hands.

"Did you two have a date?" Darwin sniggered. "I'll take good care of those flowers and you can go home."

"I'll come with you May," said Willoughby.

"No. You'll go home," said Darwin.

"Willoughby, can you message Chet?" said May.

"Of course," he said looking distraught.

Darwin drove May to Thames House, a large building on the river about twenty minutes south-west of Hoxton Hall. They went through several security checks before entering a small conference room.

"Have a seat, Ms. Abbott."

Darwin sat across from May and started looking over a few files. May was so nervous her hands started to shake.

"There is no need to be nervous Ms. Abbott. If you have nothing to hide, there is nothing to be worried about," said Darwin without looking up from her files.

May sat on her hands to try to stop the shaking. After a few minutes, Darwin closed her files and looked up at May.

"When did you first meet Sidney Beckensale?"

"Sid?" She had never heard his last name. "The first day I arrived in London. He was at Auntie Bart's house to see Chet."

"Are you aware of any plot against the United Kingdom to destroy property or harm any British citizen?"

"No, of course not."

"Have you ever met Diego Taylor?"

"No."

"Are you a member of any environmental group?"

"No."

"Have you ever participated in an environmental protest?"

"No."

"What about the pro-eco-alliance protest on Sunday."

"I wasn't participating in that," said May defensively.

Darwin pulled out another photo and placed it in front of May. The picture showed the man with the orange and brown striped sweater handing a package to Sid while May looked on.

"Why are you following me? Who took those pictures?"

Ignoring May's question, Darwin continued with her questions.

"Are you acquainted with the man in the orange and brown sweater in this photo?"

"No. That was the first time I ever saw him."

"Can you tell me what was in the package he handed Mr. Beckensale?"

"I have no idea."

"So you didn't ask your boyfriend what was in the package?"

"Sid is NOT my boyfriend. I just met him."

"Do you have a habit of kissing strangers you just meet?"

"He kissed *me*! I wasn't expecting it."

"Were you expecting this?"

Darwin pulled out another picture of Sid kissing May at the Orangery.

"Okay no more pictures. So I kissed him."

"I'm going to ask you one more time if you know what was in that package."

"I honestly have no idea!"

May could feel Darwin's eyes scrutinizing her every gesture.

"Did you know that while you were kissing lover-boy at the Orangery, a fire was started in a science lab south of the city?"

"No, I wasn't aware of that."

"That's two incidents since you arrived in this country in

which one of the main suspects is that nice bloke you've been wearing your lipstick on."

"I don't wear lipstick."

"What a convenient alibi you are. It just makes my heart swell."

Darwin sat back and let out a frustrated sigh. She opened her files again and after writing a few notes, stood up and said, "Okay. We're done."

May got up and stood facing Darwin awkwardly.

"What's going to happen now?"

"If you're telling the truth, nothing will happen. I'm going to drive you back to your Aunt Bertha's house and we'll all live happily ever after."

May grimaced at Darwin's excessive sarcasm and let out a sigh herself.

"She's not really my aunt."

"I know that," said Darwin.

As they walked to the conference room door, May asked, "Is Sid really one of the main suspects?"

Darwin just smiled politely. Then she opened the door and motioned for May to exit.

"It's time to go Ms. Abbott. I'll let you off at the end of your street so no one gets suspicious."

As they walked out, Darwin picked up Willoughby's bouquet of flowers and read the card aloud.

I hope these brighten your day as much as you brighten mine. Love, Willoughby.

"Pretty sappy if you ask me," sneered Darwin.

May grabbed the flowers from Darwin and the two got into the elevator together.

"That's two boyfriends in one trip. Busy girl."

May shot Darwin a dirty look as they exited on the main floor. Chet was waiting for her and ran over as soon as he saw her.

"Ah and here we have a third boyfriend. You sure are popular."

"Very funny," replied May.

"What exactly is this about?" he asked Darwin.

Darwin ignored Chet and turned to May.

"Do I need to give him a lift as well?"

"Yes," said May looking irritated at Darwin's comments.

The drive back to Auntie Bart's was a quiet one. When they stepped out of the car on Chet's street, Darwin looked at May gravely.

"Let's hope we don't meet again soon, Ms. Abbott."

May's mother was sitting at the kitchen table reading about the thousand-year-old castle they would be visiting in the morning.

"How was rehearsal?"

"It was great," said May feeling her stomach grumble from a combination of stress and hunger.

"Do you want some tea?"

"No thanks. Chet is taking me for ice cream. I just came by to say hello to you before we went out. We'll just be down the street."

"How nice of you, Chet. Well enjoy your ice cream."

Chet and May departed as quickly as they arrived.

"Where are we going? I'm starving," said May.

"I know a place a few blocks from here where we can talk."

CHAPTER 12

Chet, May and Reiko left the next morning in a rented car to go to Windsor Castle. After the events of the previous night, Chet decided at the last minute to come along and sat in the back seat with May. Petunia and Auntie Bart were conspicuously absent and had been since Reiko had returned, but May never asked what was said and decided not to bring up the subject. Their first stop was a West-End hotel where Reiko had arranged with Willoughby's mother to pick up Hamish. The presence of the younger boy kept Reiko occupied most of the trip as he chatted with her all the way to the town of Windsor, which they arrived at around ten a.m.

May found the town of Windsor quaint and pretty. It was filled with lovely shops, which they passed on the way to the castle. After parking the car, the four walked along a pathway that led them past a round tower and the focal point of the castle. What was once a moat filled with water surrounding the tower had been turned into beautiful gardens filled with flowers. They continued through an archway, where they came upon the main buildings of the castle. The castle was shaped like a U with a patch of grass that filled the inner space.

"On the left side of the building are the state apartments, which we can visit," said Chet.

He explained that the east wing or bottom of the building and the south wing on the right side were closed to the public because the royal residences were housed in those wings. May could see foot guards dressed in red standing at all of the entrances in front of the south wing.

"Windsor Castle is the Queen's actual home. She tries to get back to it as often as she can," said Chet.

"I wonder if she's here," said Reiko.

"No need to wonder," he said. He pointed out that the flag flying over the castle was the royal standard signaling that the Queen was in residence that day, a fact they were all very excited about.

"I can't believe she lives here," said May.

"She and loads of other people. It's the largest inhabited castle in the world. Around five hundred people live and work in it," explained Chet.

They headed left through a stone archway which brought them to the North Terrace and the entrances to the public part of the castle. The North Terrace provided a view of a vast valley and of the chapel at Eton College. They entered the north wing together, taking the tour past an enormous dollhouse that once belonged to Queen Mary, and into the main state rooms where the grandeur and beauty in each room took May's breathe away.

When they exited the building, Reiko suggested they make their way down to St. George's Chapel, which she and Hamish were interested in seeing. May wanted to enjoy the view of the valley before moving on, so she and Chet stayed back and arranged to meet Reiko and Hamish at the gift shop near the exit an hour later.

They stood quietly looking at the spring trees, reflecting on the surrounding beauty when the silence was interrupted by a loud guide behind them summoning a group to the line where a kitchen tour was supposed to start.

"Do you want to see the kitchens, May? They're actually pretty cool."

"Sure, but we'll have to tell Mom and Hamish we'll be a

little late.'

"Okay, let me go get the tickets back at the entrance and you message your mum."

Chet returned just in time for the guided tour. As the guide led them into the lower levels of the castle, he pointed out the bathroom before they entered the kitchens, and May, Chet and a few others decided to make a quick stop before rejoining the group.

"Meet me here when you're done," said Chet, disappearing behind the door to the men's bathroom.

A few minutes later May came out of her bathroom and waited for Chet. After waiting several long minutes, she started to become uneasy. The other visitors who had made a bathroom stop had already returned to the tour, and the area in front of the bathrooms was very empty and quiet.

She opened the men's bathroom door slightly and whispered Chet's name. She heard a groan and what she thought was someone being sick, and was about to run into the bathroom to help Chet when someone grabbed her arm. She turned around and saw Chet with his finger over his lips, signaling her to keep quiet. "Follow me. I found something really interesting."

She followed him down a hallway and around the corner, where there was another hallway much like the previous one. They walked to the end of the second hallway, which looked like it led to a dead end, but when they reached the far wall, Chet turned into a little nook on the righthand side that was barely noticeable. There was a small area with a few tools and some machinery lying on the ground, and it looked like people were doing some repairs.

"What is this place?" asked May.

"I don't know, but there's a guard posted here for some reason."

May looked around for a guard but didn't see anyone.

"Oh, he's in the bathroom feeling sick," explained Chet.

"Ahh, I think I heard him," said May.

"He was calling for someone to replace him when I was in

there," said Chet. "He asked for them to come quickly because he said someone absolutely had to guard this area at all times."

Tucked in the corner of the little nook was a door that was slightly ajar. Chet peeked behind the door and found a small room with a dim light in the corner and more tools and equipment on the ground. There were some old chairs and some boxes piled up in the corner.

"It doesn't look like there are any valuable items down here," said May.

"I don't think he's guarding a valuable *item*."

Chet was looking straight down at the small red carpet in the middle of the room. May looked down at the carpet and didn't notice anything unusual about it.

"Below the castle are numerous tunnels," said Chet. "Some were built hundreds of years ago so that if the castle was attacked there were ways to escape beneath."

He stepped off the carpet and pulled it away, revealing a rusted steel trapdoor with two small handles. Chet reached down and pulled on one of the handles.

"It's kind of heavy. Grab the other handle."

"Are you sure we should be doing this, Chet?"

"I just want to take a quick look."

May complied and pulled on the rusted handle, straining to lift the heavy steel. The two managed to push the trapdoor up against the adjacent wall. In the dark square opening there was a wooden ladder that descended into what looked like a deep well. Chet reached for the flashlight that was sitting on a chair and started climbing down the ladder.

"Chet, what are you doing?" May whispered nervously.

"I'm just seeing where this goes."

"Are you crazy? There will be a new guard here any minute. He'll hear us."

"I'll just be a minute."

"Chet, we can get in big trouble. Let's go back," she pleaded. But Chet kept climbing down as May stood there bewildered. He turned on a lamp that was hanging on the ladder a few steps down, revealing the bottom of the shaft and a landing area below. He climbed to the bottom then turned on his flashlight and pointed it into the tunnel. May was anxious and could feel her heart beating as she saw him disappear into the tunnel. She heard footsteps and the voices of two men in the hall.

"Chet…" May called down. "Someone's coming."

But she could no longer see him. As the voices closed in, May started panicking. There was nowhere to hide in the small room, so she slipped down the ladder as quietly as possible just as the two men walked into the room. She heard them complaining about the workers having left the trapdoor open and the light on. When she reached the bottom of the ladder, she moved into the tunnel so they wouldn't see her if they looked down the shaft. She could see the light from Chet's flashlight down the tunnel but didn't call to him in case she was heard. She wanted to run toward him, but the space in between them was pitch black, and she was scared she would lose her footing. She could hear muffled voices above but could no longer make out exactly what the men were saying. It occurred to her that the men might close the trapdoor, and in that instant she started running toward Chet's light. The quiet in the tunnel was so intense that it was heavy in her ears as she ran. She could hardly hear her own footsteps. She whispered Chet's name but he didn't turn around. She felt the ancient air against her skin and the musty smell in her nose. The dark was so oppressive, she felt like she'd been pulled into a black hole. She focused on the light from Chet's flashlight and stumbled toward it.

"Chet!" she cried as she finally came upon the light. It was so dark, she couldn't even make out his body, and it looked like a hand was walking alone with a flashlight. Chet jumped at the sound of her voice and turned around quickly, pointing the flashlight in her eyes.

"You scared the heck out of me, May."

"I scared the heck out of YOU?" she said, raising her voice loud enough that it startled them both. "Chet, there were two men talking in the room and they could be closing the trapdoor and we'll be stuck down here forever. We could die down here. And I'm going to be in so much trouble. I'm going to wish I had died down here!"

"Look," he said, pointing his flashlight farther down the tunnel to where there appeared to be an opening in the ceiling. May got a good glimpse of the semicircular tunnel for the first time as he pointed his flashlight into it. It was what Chet would later tell her was limestone, with rough rocks jutting out from around the arched shape and crumbled pieces of rocks gathering on each side of the tunnel floor.

Chet walked toward the opening and May clutched his arm. The opening was a shaft that looked similar to the one they had climbed down a few minutes before. It had a ladder, which, like the previous ladder, had a lamp halfway up. Chet handed May his flashlight and started climbing up. When he reached the halfway point, he turned on the lamp, revealing an identical square steel trap door. He pushed on the trapdoor and it moved upwards but was blocked by something. He pushed harder and the trapdoor landed on its flipside with a dull thud on top of the rug that was covering it. May looked up at the light and felt a deep sense of relief. She started climbing up the ladder and reached Chet's feet within a few seconds. He had stopped to peek out of the top and see if the coast was clear. Then he climbed out of the small opening. May climbed out immediately after him, finding herself in a room that looked like an administrative office. There was a small desk with some papers, pens, and a mug on it. On the wall was a calendar with vintage cars on it, and in the corner was a tiny fireplace. Without talking they quietly replaced the trapdoor and covered it with the carpet. Their shoes were full of dust from the tunnel, which had left footprints on the carpet. After cleaning their shoes and their prints from the floor with their hands, Chet walked toward the large office door and gently turned the handle. He peeked out and gestured for May to follow him. She peeked out instinctively before stepping out into a long, narrow corridor that looked similar to the one in the basement of her school. It was modern by the castle's thousand-year-old standards but was painted in a plain off-white that looked dated by modern standards. The corridor was quiet and empty and they walked along its tiled floor until they reached a stairwell leading up.

"This should take us to the main floor," said Chet, and he started up the stairwell, moving quickly. But May stood still and was looking up at a sign on the wall.

Chet stopped and turned back as if he sensed that May was not following him.

"Are you coming, May?"

"There's a fire exit sign here, Chet. The exit is down this hall. Let's get out of here."

Chet looked at her contemplatively as if gauging her tolerance for risk, and said, "If my internal compass is correct, we're on the other side of the castle. We have to go upstairs to check it out."

"You've got to be kidding."

"May, it's the chance of a lifetime," he implored. "Have you ever heard of the term *carpe diem*?"

May couldn't even answer. She was flabbergasted that he wanted to continue with this reckless adventure.

"It's Latin. It means *seize the day*."

"I know what it means," said May dryly.

"Come on, then."

"No way, Chet. I'm finding the exit and running. I *have* been seizing the day! If I do any more seizing, I'm going to end up in jail. I already have your security service after me."

"You're going to get in trouble if you run out an exit door. There are guards everywhere. We might as well look around for a few minutes."

May felt sick. He was right. They were trapped until they could figure something out.

"My mother's going to strangle me if I get caught. Going to jail might be a holiday."

"I'll think of a way out. I promise," he said. "You said I was such a bore. I'm just trying to make the trip more exciting for you," said Chet with amusement, trying to lighten the mood.

May glared at him.

"Come on. We'll find a way out," said Chet.

May, suddenly feeling exhausted and figuring that she was doomed anyway, gave in and followed Chet. They walked up the stairs and through a door, coming out into a long, grand corridor lined with large windows, fine pieces of furniture, and several magnificent paintings.

"Where are we?" May asked.

Chet pointed out of the window and smiled. "Look outside," he said.

"You were right. We're on the other side of the castle," said May.

"We're in the east wing, which is closed off to visitors."

"Shouldn't some sort of alarm be going off?" asked May.

"Let's hope not," said Chet.

"This place in incredible," whispered May as she followed him closely.

She realized, even through her terror, that she was experiencing something incredibly rare. They walked quietly along the enormous corridor passing ornate vases, stunning sculptures, a beautiful fireplace, and the most impressive grandfather clock she had ever seen. Her fear and anxiety subsided a bit and she felt herself getting lost in the beauty and splendor that surrounded her. She was astounded by the elaborate workmanship of the walls and ceilings.

"It's spectacular." she said, forgetting how agitated she had been a minute ago.

"Amazing," he replied.

"Chet?"

"Yes, May?"

"What's that noise?"

Chet stopped walking and listened for the sound.

"I just heard something. I think it came from the end of the corridor," said May. "It sounded like a voice."

"I didn't hear anything," said Chet.

May stood still, unable to move.

"Chet, let's find an exit and get out of here."

"Okay, there should be one right here at the end of the hall."

They crept along the corridor as quietly as they could.

"I just heard it again," said May. "It was a woman's voice. I'm sure of it. It sounded as if she was chanting something."

"I heard it too this time. I can't tell if it's coming from behind us or ahead of us though. The acoustics are strange in this hall."

May thought the voice sounded distressed.

"The second wife of Henry VIII, Anne Boleyn, is said to haunt the halls of Windsor Castle," said Chet in a whisper that was barely audible.

"You mean the one whose head he had chopped off?" asked May in an even quieter whisper.

"He had a couple wives beheaded, but yes, she was one of them."

"This is really not a good time for humour."

"I'm not joking. Guests who've stayed at the castle have heard her."

May felt the hair on the back of her neck stand up. She started walking faster, and Chet, feeling her sense of urgency, kept her pace. They came to an archway where they expected to find an exit but instead found several large doors.

"How do we get out of here?" asked May, feeling the panic start to rise.

"Okay, calm down. Just follow me. There has to be an exit close by."

"I think we should turn around," said May.

They had stopped and faced each other for a moment, trying to decide which way to go, when a voice chimed out from outside one of the doors.

"What wilt thou do? Thou wilt not murder me? Help, help, ho."

The archway was dark and May clapped her hand over her mouth to stifle a scream. May's eyes grew wide with fear as she listened for the voice.

"O me, what hast thou done?" asked the voice.

Chet and May looked at each other and understanding

started to spread over their faces.

May was now shaking uncontrollably, but she instinctively started walking toward the room from which the haunting voice emanated, and she stood in front of the large door.

"May, what are you doing?" whispered Chet. "Let's get out of here."

"HAMLET" was the only word that came out of May's mouth.

The word came out louder than May expected, and the voice behind the door was suddenly quiet.

"*Who's there?*" the voice inquired.

May and Chet stood there in disbelief and horror, but before they could regain their composure, they looked down and saw the doorknob turning. May's legs felt like lead, frozen by the sheer terror of what was about to happen. All she could do was stand motionless and helpless as the door opened. Then before them stood a woman with an inquisitive look on her face. It took them several seconds to process who was standing before them. Both of their mouths were wide open as they stood before Queen Elizabeth II.

"You may catch a fly in those mouths if you keep them open any longer," said the Queen.

"So sorry, Your Majesty," they chimed.

Chet bowed and May, taking his cue, gave a quick curtsy.

"Are you lost?"

"No, Your Majesty. I mean, sort of, Your Majesty," said May.

They looked at each other uneasily, trying to assess the situation.

"I'm Chester T. Yorke and this is May B. Abbott," said Chet formally, trying to extinguish the awkward moment of silence and surprising May with his memory of her middle initial from their first meeting.

"Pleased to make your acquaintance," responded the Queen guardedly.

She looked at May curiously and said, "You knew that I was reciting lines from *Hamlet*, young lady. Do you like

Shakespeare?"

"Yes, Your Majesty."

"You're lucky you weren't here twenty minutes ago when I practicing my very poor Yorkshire accent," she said, looking directly at Chet.

"I don't know about your Yorkshire accent but from the little I heard, you seem to be a natural at Shakespeare," said May.

May wasn't sure she was supposed to speak to the Queen of England without being addressed by her first and now turned red with embarrassment, wondering whether she had made a blunder.

"Reciting lines helps keep my voice nimble. I especially love Shakespeare."

"May is playing Ophelia in *Hamlet* on Saturday at the Shakespeare Globe Theatre. Professor Winterbottom told us you might attend if your calendar permits, Your Majesty," said Chet.

"Yes, Ruth Winterbottom. I remember her hair well," the Queen said with an almost imperceptible chuckle. "I will indeed be in attendance."

She turned to May and said, "I recognize your accent. Are you from Canada, Ms. Abbott?"

"Yes I am, ma'am."

"I have always been so fond of Canada. My mother was a great lover of the land as well. What does the B stand for in your name, Ms. Abbott?"

May, suddenly looking completely mortified, said in a barely audible voice, "Bungo."

Without missing a beat, Queen Elizabeth said, "Ah, how nice. Well, you best get going. I shall walk you back to the exit myself. I do think the footguards will be quite displeased if they find you walking around alone."

Then she stopped and looked at them seriously. Her eyes were firm, and May knew they were in front of a great and strong woman.

"I trust that you will keep today's events to yourself."

Her tone was kind and soft but firm, and she elicited a reverence May had never experienced.

"Of course, ma'am," they both chimed.

They walked down the long corridor slowly.

"How do you like this corridor?" asked the Queen, her tone once again easy and gregarious. "It's one of my favourites."

"It's extraordinary," replied May.

"Magnificent, Your Majesty," added Chet.

"Quite something, isn't it? I'm glad you like it. It's a rare treat for you to see it. It's not open to the public," she said with a raised eyebrow that May didn't miss.

The Queen guided them to an exit they hadn't noticed before and opened it slightly. The guard watching the door was taken aback by the Queen's unexpected presence and bowed to her at once.

"Can you please escort these two back to the public area."

"Is everything alright, Your Majesty?" asked the guard.

"Everything is fine. Thank you."

As the door began to shut the Queen said, "Ms. Abbott, I'm sure you shall make a fine Ophelia. Good luck to you both."

The guard looked at them suspiciously as he escorted them out of the exit that led them back to the courtyard. Several tourists, seeing them coming out of the private residences, gathered around them trying to figure out who they were before shrugging and wandering off as May and Chet walked briskly toward St. George's Chapel. When they were halfway there, May felt someone walking beside her rather closely.

"I don't want to draw any undue attention in this place, Ms. Abbott, so I suggest you and your little friend follow me."

May looked over to see Darwin Lee keeping pace beside her. Beside Chet was a man in a black suit. The four of them walked right past where they were to meet Reiko and Hamish and entered an administration building in the Horseshoe Cloister.

CHAPTER 13

Darwin led May into one office and her colleague led Chet into another.

"Have a seat Ms. Abbott."

May sat down across from Darwin feeling less nervous than the last time. In fact, she was becoming extremely annoyed at how difficult Darwin was making her life.

"Two people go missing from a kitchen tour in the castle that the Queen lives in while the whole country is on high alert and guess who I find?"

"Nice to see you too, Agent Lee."

"What exactly are you two doing here, Ms. Abbott?"

"What a lot of tourists do when they visit London. Just taking a side trip to Windsor Castle. What are *you* doing here, Agent Lee? A little sightseeing or are you just following me per usual. Things a little slow down at MI5 headquarters?" asked May.

May detected a hint of surprise in Darwin's expression at May's defiant tone.

"As you may have gathered, we are exploring possible threats to the Queen. Seems we found one quicker than we imagined."

"You know as well as I do that I'm not a threat."

"How did you infiltrate the Queen's residence?"

"Infiltrate? We kind of got lost. My friend Chet found a

passage and we followed it. We didn't know we were in the Queen's residence until we saw her."

"They really have to close up that passageway. Did you exchange any words with Her Majesty?"

"No."

"You're a terrible liar."

"I take that as a compliment."

Darwin sighed, frustrated by May's insubordination.

"You don't have authorization to question me, do you?" said May.

"I'm working on it," replied Darwin. "I would just like to know what you discussed with the Queen."

"What I discussed with the Queen is private."

Darwin threw up her arms.

"This case is driving me crazy!"

"That's because you are looking in the wrong place. I'm just a regular teenager from Toronto, not a threat to national security."

Darwin reached into her bag and pulled out a photo. May grimaced at the prospect of another picture of her kissing Sid but instead was presented with a picture of a blond man with a large scar on his face.

"Have you ever seen this man?"

"Actually, yes. I noticed him at the Orangery when I was having tea with Sid. It was his scar that got my attention."

"I gave him that scar a couple years ago," said Darwin. "Pretty gruesome isn't it? It was the most fun I had that whole year." She let out a slight giggle exposing a set of perfect teeth. May thought she might actually be attractive if she wasn't so diabolically unpleasant.

"His name is Jet Jango," continued Darwin. "He works for *Dish-Now-Britain* and he's been covering the terrorist attacks. He's a sensational, *make-it-up-as-you-go-along* hack with no morals. Ex-boyfriend."

"He's your ex-boyfriend?"

"I'm not sure whether he's pursuing this case because he wants to cover the eco-terrorism story or because he's still attracted to me. Either way, he's just dying to print something that isn't true about all of us to ruin our lives. Avoid him like the plague and whatever you do, don't talk to him. He'll twist your words around. He's a snake who would sell his mother for publicity. A real tosser. He followed you here."

"He followed me here?"

"And I followed him here. I just confiscated his camera. Second one this week. I just took a quick look at. He's got a whole lot of pictures of you on there. Can't wait to take a closer look at those."

May was alarmed that this reporter was following her and thought about what her mother would say if those pictures were printed. Her mother! May stood up suddenly.

"Can I go now? My mother is going to kill me."

Darwin looked at May for a long time.

"Just wait a minute while I talk to my colleague."

Darwin left the room for a few minutes and May checked the time on her father's phone. She was an hour late and her mother had tried to call her several times. As she put the phone in her pocket, she noticed that Darwin had left her notebook lying open on the desk. May grabbed it quickly and started flipping through the pages frantically. She found a photo of Darwin in a bikini tucked between the back page. On the back of the photo was a hand written note that said, *Miss you baby. Love Jet.*

"Ewe," she said aloud.

She replaced the picture and continued to look at recent notes. Among the illegible scribbles, May noticed a name in bold that she recognized immediately. *Sid.* Written below his name was:

The Meeting Room
Friday nights: 11:00 pm – 4:00 am

There was an address next to the time which May quickly wrote on her arm with a pen that was lying on the desk.

May could hear Darwin walking back and quickly put the notebook back where she found it. When Darwin came in, she pulled out a business card and handed it to May.

"Call me if there is anything you feel the need to tell me."

May put Darwin's business card in her pocket and walked swiftly out of the room. Chet was waiting for her and the two ran to St. George's chapel where they met a pale and worried-looking Reiko. May made up a story about how they were not allowed out of the kitchens because of a security breach and how they'd tried to call but their phones didn't work in the kitchens because they were below ground. Her mother had seen several security personnel in the area, and though she looked slightly unconvinced, she didn't question May any further.

On the way back to London, May and Chet sat in the back seat of the car and tried to talk discreetly. Thankfully, Reiko was preoccupied with driving on the opposite side of the road and the constant chatter of Hamish.

"So Darwin's colleague didn't ask you anything about Sid?"

"Nope. We just talked about sports. We had a pleasant chat. Nice bloke," said Chet.

When they arrived back in London, Reiko dropped Hamish off at his hotel and May and Chet off at Professor Winterbottom's house. Chet had promised Reiko he would accompany May that evening for rehearsal so there would be someone to come back with her to Auntie Bart's house. Rehearsal with Tucker went so well, they were done in a little over an hour.

When they got back to Auntie Bart's, Chet mentioned that Hannah had messaged him confirming that she was out of the hospital, infection free and was looking forward to hosting them for breakfast at her house the following morning.

They got up early on Friday and headed to the Frost residence, where Hannah lived on a quiet, tree-lined street in the west end. A tall gentleman wearing a navy blue suit and a bowtie with white, thick, wavy hair and matching eyebrows answered the door and welcomed them into a big hall. His teeth were pearly white, and he was slightly tanned.

"Nice to see you kids. Come on in. No need to take your

shoes off."

The man beckoned them to follow him down the wide hallway. Hannah's house was decorated in beautiful rich colors and traditional stylings with opulent rugs and decorative lamps. As they made their way toward the large, winding wooden staircase that split the hall in two, the gentleman with the white hair turned to them and said, "Knock, knock."

May and Chet looked at each other, a little puzzled.

"Come on, kids, humour me! KNOCK, KNOCK," repeated the man.

"Who's there?" replied May softly, unsure if he was actually trying to tell a joke.

"Boo," said the man.

"Boo who?" answered May.

"Now, don't cry dear, Hannah will be down in a second."

Chet and May couldn't help but laugh at the gentleman's antics.

"DAD!" yelled a voice from above them.

Hannah was standing at the top of the staircase with her hand on her forehead as if she were in grave pain.

"Well, good morning, Pumpkin," replied the man.

"DAD, THEY'RE NOT SIX YEARS OLD. PLEASE DON'T TELL THEM KNOCK-KNOCK JOKES," yelled Hannah.

"Oh, come now, Pumpkin. They thought it was funny. Didn't you kids?"

Chet said, "Yes, sir. Good one."

"Hilarious," mirrored May, feeling sorry for the fact that Hannah had yelled at him.

"Let me know if you need anything," said Hannah's father. "Don't be shy. My home is your home."

He seemed so jovial and good-natured, May couldn't imagine how he could be Hannah's father. Hannah, who was still standing at the top of the staircase, looked like she was going to be ill.

"Dad, can you just have breakfast sent up."

"Certainly, darling. Right away."

Hannah summoned May and Chet up the stairs and led them down a grand hallway lined with intricate wooden paneling and colourful artwork. She was on crutches and it took her a while to move along the hallway.

"My dad wasn't supposed to be around. I had no idea he was taking the morning off work. He's one of those parents who think they're funny when they're actually an embarrassment to themselves. It's mortifying."

"I thought he was pretty cool," said May, feeling she had to defend such a nice man.

They snailed their way up a second flight of stairs, following Hannah through a glass door onto a beautiful patio filled with flowers, comfortable couches and a table.

"Have a seat," said Hannah.

A lady came up and laid down a tray full of warm scones and some tea.

They drank and ate until Willoughby showed up a few minutes later.

"Sorry I'm late. I was talking to the butler. What a hilarious fellow."

"Yeah—the *butler* is just a boatload of fun," replied Hannah, rolling her eyes.

"My brother Hamish is still talking to him," said Willoughby.

"Your brother is here?" asked Chet.

"Sorry, I promised him I'd bring him to rehearsal today." Willoughby grabbed a butterscotch scone, took a huge bite out of it then turned to Hannah. "So what did you find out, princess?"

Hannah leaned forward, looking grave. "The hooligan was here on Tuesday evening. I told my mother to let it slip that I found him attractive to make sure he'd show up. Like I would have a thing for someone like him. He *wishes* he was in my league. Men are such gullible morons." Hannah let out a snigger and Chet shifted uncomfortably in his seat.

"Does the hooligan have a name?" asked May.

"Oh, it's Koole. Ha! Can you believe it? His mother should

129

have made his middle name *I wish*."

Hannah threw back her head in laughter and her face began to look awkward and purplish.

"I've never actually seen her laugh," said Willoughby in wonder. "It's making me nervous."

It took a couple minutes for Hannah to compose herself. She seemed out of breath, as if laughing was a chore. When she was finally calm, she leaned in towards her audience dramatically.

"Well," she continued, "Koole told me all about the group he has been involved with. It's the same one that your friend Sid is associating himself with, under Diego Taylor who Koole says is absolutely mad. Diego considers himself an environmental vigilante. Saving the Earth is a personal vendetta."

May, Chet and Willoughby exchanged glances.

"Sid told me a bit about Diego," said Chet.

"I did more research on him. He's been quoted as saying that moderate environmental groups are not doing enough and need to take a more radical approach."

"Did he recruit Koole from one of these moderate groups?" asked Chet.

"Actually, no," said Hannah. "This is the scary part. Koole was being paid for his services."

"Paid?"

"Diego pays Koole and a couple others who couldn't care less about the environment but will do a lot of the risky and dirty work if the money's right. And from what I understand from Koole, Diego makes it worth everyone's while."

"So he hires environmental mercenaries?" asked Chet.

"Looks that way," said Hannah.

"How can Diego afford to do that? Where does he get the funding?" asked May.

"Most of the money comes from Diego himself. His father was a very wealthy businessman from South America. His mother was an American environmentalist who had cancer. They both died in a plane crash on their way to a treatment centre in the United States. He uses his mother's last name," said Hannah.

"Do you think he's paying Sid?" ask May.

"No. Koole said he pays very few people. Sid is actually part of Diego's inner circle. Sid's there because he believes in what Diego is doing."

"The government has considered eco-terrorism a serious threat to national security for a long time," said Willoughby

"And Diego Taylor's is at the top of their watch list these days. Most reputable environmental groups have distanced themselves from him in the past few months. I don't blame them. So many people are doing such good work for the environment in a peaceful manner," she said. "And these few nutters have to ruin it for everyone."

"I thought you said you didn't care about the environment?" growled Willoughby.

"I never said that," said Hannah.

"You said you didn't care if all the fish dropped dead in the sea,"

"You take everything so literally."

"So litera...? Wha...?" Willoughby looked incensed. "You said you were only concerned about your flawless skin!"

"I do have flawless skin, don't I? I'm glad you noticed. Can I finish what I was saying, or are you going to continue to yell at me?"

"I'm not yelling at you," said Willoughby, glowering. "Scottish people just have loud voices."

"Here's the interesting part," continued Hannah. "A fire in a research facility was set a couple month ago and a lady was hurt. I'm sure you heard about it. Well, Koole was one of the hooligans who set fire to the place. MI5 approached him, saying they knew he was guilty and that because of the injured lady, he'd be going to jail for a long time unless he decided to work for them covertly. They knew he felt no loyalty to the cause so he was a perfect spy. Of course he accepted. He told me something is going down at the Globe Theatre on Saturday night and Sid is definitely involved."

"Are you sure?" asked May have trouble accepting the truth about Sid.

"Did he say what was going to happen?" asked Chet.

"He couldn't tell me but with the Queen and other members of the royal family attending, who knows. They could be planning on kidnapping her or something. Or blowing up the place."

"I can't imagine they would go that far," said Chet.

"You said yourself that Sid discussed taking care of HRH with some suspicious blonde girl at the hospital."

"I don't remember saying she looked suspicious," said Chet.

"She sounded suspicious to me," scoffed Hannah. "I mean, she was dressed fashionably right? And Sid dresses … well …"

"Why would they target the Queen?" asked May ignoring Hannah's comment.

"To get the world's attention, I suppose," answered Willoughby.

"There will be way too much security around the Queen. They wouldn't be able to get near her. Plus, they wouldn't be making any friends by picking on her. It doesn't make sense," said Chet.

"Somehow I don't think they're looking to make friends," said Willoughby. "What are we going to do now? Should we tell Uncle Hamilton that Sid is involved in something serious?"

Hamish walked into the room at that moment and blurted out, "To tell or not to tell. That is the question." He turned to face them dramatically. "When I'm faced with life's questions, I always ask myself what Rosencrantz and Guildenstern would do in the same situation."

Hannah looked at him with disdain and said, "Rosencrantz and Guildenstern?"

"Do you *not* know who Rosencrantz and Guildenstern are? They're Hamlet's friends and confidants. Considering you go to a prominent school, your level of education is questionable. Your parents should ask for their money back."

"I know who Rosencrantz and Guildenstern are! Why am I

even talking to you?" said Hannah, infuriated.

"You must find me attractive on some level."

Hannah's jaw dropped and her face was filled with disgust. "Willoughby can you get this little brat out of here."

"Brat? Is that all I get? One sole NOUN? So disappointing. I need adjectives for my life to have meaning. I'm not a Hemingway novel. I think a *treacherous brat* would be more fitting. In fact, the word brat is in itself rather weak. I like scoundrel or miscreant. So much more romantic. You really need to work on your vocabulary. People will never take you seriously, especially with those gut-wrenching good looks."

"Does this kid ever shut up?" asked Hannah.

"Very rarely," said Willoughby.

Willoughby grabbed his brother by the arm and escorted him to the patio door and told him to wait for them downstairs."

"We've got to get going Hannah," said Chet. "Good work. That's a lot of information for Koole to tell you. You really got him to talk," said Chet.

"Well it wasn't free. There was some payment involved," explained Hannah.

The three of them looked alarmed.

"How exactly did you pay him?" asked Chet.

"Rumour is that Sid and Diego are pretty tight, but Sid is quite a slippery one. He keeps a low profile and they have trouble tracking him at certain times. Sid doesn't trust Koole and will not respond to any of his attempts to communicate so Koole asked me to put a GPS tracking device on him. Koole overheard someone at MI5 say that Sid's phone is always turned off so tracking him is impossible at times. Koole thought it would get him some brownie points if he could track Sid's every movement."

"WHAT?" cried Chet.

"Isn't that against the law?" asked May.

"I told you she couldn't be trusted," said Willoughby.

"How were you able to get a hold of him?" ask Chet.

"My father has an old vintage guitar he's been wanting to

sell. It was owned by some famous blues guy who I've never heard of. I messaged Sid's vocal teacher and asked her to pass along the message to Sid. He came straight away and purchased it. Not sure where he got that kind of money."

Chet looked at Hannah in disbelief.

"I put two devices on him," she continued. "One on that ridiculous leather jacket he always wears, which he had taken off, and one in his new guitar case."

"You're joking right? I'm messaging him right now," said Chet.

"That won't work. Like I said, Sid has apparently become super paranoid about being tracked through the GPS on his phone. It will probably be off."

"Why would you do that, Hannah?" asked Chet.

"You wanted me to get information for you," she said defensively. "I thought you'd be happy. You didn't think Koole would give me information for nothing, do you? He said he wouldn't tell me anything until I agreed to at least try to meet Sid. The more information Koole has on Diego's inner circle, the better. He's thinking they might make him an intelligence agent if he is able to prove himself."

"Koole sounds delusional. And I can't believe you did that," cried Chet. "Sid is our friend."

"A friend who is potentially involved in a plot to kidnap the Queen and who knows what else."

"Hannah, there's no concrete evidence to support that," said May, finally chiming in.

"If he's not guilty then you have nothing to worry about," said Hannah.

"I knew we shouldn't have told her about Sid at the hospital," repeated Willoughby.

"He might be planning to blow up the Globe Theatre while we're watching the play for all we know," cried Hannah.

"That's ridiculous," said Chet. "Sid's not going to blow anything up!"

"You don't know that. This is serious stuff. I figured I was doing a public service, frankly," she said belligerently. "Plus

Koole was surprised when I told him about the package that Sid received at the demonstration so maybe there's a plan even he doesn't know about."

"You told him about the package?" said Chet furiously. "Listen, we have to go. Willow and May are going to be late for dress rehearsal. And I have to find Sid."

Willoughby shot Hannah a disgusted look and stormed out of the room after Chet. May got up to follow but Hannah grabbed her arm discreetly as she tried to leave and softly said, "May, can I speak with you alone for a moment?"

CHAPTER 14

Chet, Willoughby, and Hamish were waiting outside Hannah's door when May caught up with them a few minutes later, and they all headed to the Globe Theatre. When they arrived, they were greeted by a heavy contingent of security and were asked to produce special passes given to all students by Professor Winterbottom. Although it was only dress rehearsal, security checked everyone and everything that came into and out of the theatre. Hamish didn't have a pass and Willoughby had to spend several minutes convincing the security guard that his younger brother was not a threat to national security. When they got into the theatre, Willoughby went straight backstage to start changing for dress rehearsal, dragging his brother along. The backstage area of the theatre was a large wooden room traditionally called the "tiring house." There were three doors leading out to the stage: a large one in the middle, and two smaller ones on each side.

Chet told May he was going to look around the Globe to see if he could find Sid. May said she needed to speak with Winterbottom and would be along shortly. May was speaking with one of the stewards when Chet reappeared by her side. Stewards were volunteers whose duty it was to help usher people to their seats, provide patrons with information, and maintain general order in the theatre. May introduced the steward as Ray. He was a short, stocky bald man with dark circles around his eyes that made him look somewhat like a bald raccoon. He had abnormally large lips that thinned out when he smiled, which was often. He was friendly and jovial and laughed heartily, and the traditional red steward's suit made him look like a short Santa Claus when he laughed. Rae told them about some of the memorable plays he had seen over the years and some of the great actors he had met. Chet asked him about the security as nonchalantly as possible, and Rae told them he'd never seen anything like it in all the years he'd volunteered there.

"With the Royals coming, they are taking every precaution," said Rae. "We've been going over protocols for the Queen's visit all week. They've searched the place and are watching everyone and everything coming into the theatre, especially with everything that's been going on in the city lately," he added.

May and Chet exchanged uncomfortable glances and May changed the subject quickly by turning to Chet and saying, "Rae showed me where the party is going to be held tomorrow night after the play. There's a fantastic room downstairs with an oak tree in the middle of the room."

"I've seen the room before. It's called the UnderGlobe," said Chet. "It's where the tours start. Apparently some students are decorating it for tomorrow's party."

"I'm sure it will be a really fun party for you kids," said Rae, adding that he'd love to stay to chat some more but was expected at a meeting with the other stewards. When Rae left to attend to his duties, Chet asked May if she had seen Sid.

"No. I guess you didn't see him either," she replied.

"I can't believe I am not able to get a hold of my best friend. I have sent him messages via every possible method. This is ridiculous."

"Let's head backstage to see Willoughby," said May. "Maybe he's seen him or heard something."

The tiring house was bursting with activity and students

were tripping over costumes and putting on makeup. Most of the girls were doing their own makeup but Willoughby was sitting in a chair with a handkerchief around his head, and a pretty lady in jeans and a white T-shirt was applying mascara to his eyelashes.

"Nice lashes, Willow," Chet chuckled as they stopped in front of the makeup table.

"It apparently makes my eyes look dramatic onstage," said Willoughby.

Willoughby kept turning his head as he spoke, and the makeup artist kept telling him to stop moving.

"Where is your brother?"

"The little twit is taking a nap in the upper level stands."

As he finished his sentence he whipped his head around toward May, knocking down lipsticks and other make-up.

"May?"

"Yes?"

"Why aren't you in costume?"

Chet stopped and turned to May inquisitively.

"Yeah, May, what's going on?"

"Oh, right. I meant to tell you. I'm out of the play," she said matter-of-factly.

Chet and Willoughby stood frozen for several seconds.

"I don't understand. Is this some sort of joke?" asked Chet.

"No joke," said May. "I just confirmed with Professor Winterbottom. I'm not allowed to be in the play."

Willoughby and Chet stood flabbergasted for several more seconds, unable to say anything while May continued. "Tucker mentioned something about me at the dinner table, and his dad complained about the fact that I didn't attend the school."

"That rat. I'm going to beat him to a pulp," said Chet.

"Calm down, Chet," said May. "It's not his fault. He was really upset as well, not only about me not being in the play but about his sister replacing me."

"His *sister* is playing Ophelia?" said Willoughby.

"Yes. Her name is Blanche. She takes acting lessons and has had small parts in some recent films. She's been rehearsing with Tucker every night to help him out, so she knows the lines. She goes to Hannah's school. Hannah said Blanche was too young to audition, but they're making an exception for her. Apparently she's really good," said May.

"When did you speak with Hannah? Is she the one who told you?" asked Chet.

"Yes—she told this morning right before we left her house."

"That snake!" yelled Willoughby.

"Willoughby, I actually think Hannah felt pretty bad. She only told me because she didn't want me to be blindsided when I got here this morning."

"A brother and sister playing Hamlet and Ophelia is disgusting!" said Willoughby.

"They're just acting," said May calmly.

Chet let out a sympathetic sigh and said, "I'm so sorry, May."

"Me too, May," echoed Willoughby, his rage subsiding for a moment. "How can you be so calm about this?"

May wasn't sure what the answer was but she wasn't as upset as she'd imagined she would be. A couple of days ago she might have been devastated, but she didn't feel that way now. She couldn't quite explain it but she felt comforted, even empowered knowing she would have actually gone through with it. After contemplating these things quietly, she looked up and realized that the two boys were staring at her intently, waiting for an answer.

"I'm just grateful for having been a part of it," she finally said. "I actually feel a little bad for Tucker," she continued. "I bumped into him earlier and he seems really upset."

"Did the rat apologize?" asked Willoughby.

"No, but I think he feels bad down deep."

Willoughby's left eyebrow went up, then he smiled at May. "You really see the best in people, don't you?" He put his hand on her shoulder.

"It's very Canadian, May," laughed Chet, patting her fondly on the back.

The room started emptying out and was suddenly quiet after Professor Winterbottom had come around to tell everyone that they were starting dress rehearsal. Willoughby gathered his things and put them in a pile in the corner of the room, and May and Chet walked down the stage stairs into the yard.

"Did Hannah say she was coming to the actual play tomorrow?" asked Chet as they sat on a wooden bench.

"Yes, she and her parents are coming," replied May.

Chet just grimaced and changed the subject. "Did you want to stay to watch the dress rehearsal?" he asked.

"Yes, of course!" she said.

"Are you sure there isn't something else in London you want to see? You only have a couple of days left and I don't really need to be here. I can take you anywhere you want to go."

The week had gone by so quickly. She couldn't believe she was leaving to go back home in two days. Though there were a few things she wanted to see, right now May didn't want to be anywhere else but at the Globe. They watched the dress rehearsal and she was surprised at how smoothly it went, and how natural Tucker and his sister Blanche looked. When rehearsal was over, they went backstage to the tiring house where the cast was chatting loudly, getting changed and removing makeup. May snuck through the tiring house doors and stepped out onto the stage, which was now empty save for a few props. She looked up at the sky and remembered the wonder she felt the first time she was in the theatre only a few days ago. A while later Chet peeked out onto the stage.

"Ah, here you are," he said.

"I just wanted to take it all in," said May. "This is very likely the last time I will ever get to stand on this stage. It's a great view."

The two of them lay down on their backs on the stage for a long time, looking straight up at the early evening sky until it became very quiet.

"I think everyone is gone. You don't think they'll lock us

in, do you?" said May.

"That would be great," said Chet.

May smiled. "I'm going into the stands to see the view from up there."

They climbed to the top rafters and leaned over the railing.

"We should go. I need to go to Uncle Hamilton's to warn Sid about Hannah's tracker."

"Good idea."

"Let's go grab some ice cream on the way," said Chet.

"I was wondering when I'd get that ice cream you promised me."

As they started heading toward the stairs, they saw a hooded man peek through the trap door in the middle of the stage. The man looked around surreptitiously and signaled to someone below him who also climbed out of the opening in the stage. The two men walked briskly down the stage stairs toward the exit at the other side of the yard without noticing Chet and May looking down on them from the stands. Though they couldn't see either of their faces, May and Chet recognized the distinct walk and lean figure of Sid. Instinctively, and without saying a word to each other, they both started making their way down the stairs. But by the time they made it down into the yard and out the exit, the two men were already on the other side of the outdoor piazza and walking through the gate that led out into the street. Chet began running and was catching up as the two men entered an awaiting van that screeched away as soon as they shut the door behind them. When Chet got to the street, he was left standing in front of two security guards who were guarding the gate. May caught up with him a few seconds later and the two of them stood on the street looking toward where the van had just disappeared. The two security guards looked at Chet and May suspiciously.

"Can we help you?" said one of the guards.

"No. That's okay. We were just leaving," said May as she grabbed Chet's arm and pulled him away from the theatre.

Chet looked at May strangely.

"Don't you think we should report that to security?"

"I'm going to call Agent Lee."

May pulled out Darwin's card and dialed the number on her father's phone.

"Miss me already, Ms. Abbott?"

"Not really. But thanks for asking."

"What can I do for you?"

"I just saw two hooded men coming out of the trap door leading beneath the stage at the Globe Theatre."

"Go on."

"Well, I just found it suspicious."

"Why would you find that suspicious? Maybe they were maintenance men."

"They were *not* maintenance men."

"I see," said Agent Lee. "And did you recognize either of the men?"

"No," lied May.

There was a long pause.

"You are sure you didn't recognize either of them?"

"Yes, I'm sure."

"I see. Is that all, Ms. Abbott?"

"Yes."

"I'll look into it. Thank you for the call."

May hung up and felt sick.

"She knows it was Sid."

"You did the right thing, May. I feel just as bad. He's my best friend but our families are going to be there tomorrow night. The Queen is going to be there!"

"I know," said May dejectedly. "Let's go home.".

CHAPTER 15

Things seemed to be smoothed over somewhat between Reiko and Petunia, so there was a lot less tension in the house. Chet grabbed a bite to eat and then went to Hammer Dog's to see if Sid was there. When he left, Reiko asked May if they could talk privately.

"Sure. Why don't we go for a walk," said May.

They strolled down several streets, admiring the charming row houses and pretty gardens. The sun had set and the evening air penetrated May's flimsy sweater. She was terrified her mother was going to ask her questions about Chet or Sid and braced herself for the worst, but Reiko affectionately put her arm around her and said, "Petunia is not coming back to Canada."

"Oh."

"Petunia thinks you are too old for a nanny and she really wants to stay in London." Reiko paused for a few moments, allowing the news to sink in for both of them. "I've known that for a long time."

"That Petunia wants to move back to London?" asked May.

"No, that you no longer need a nanny."

May had never really thought of Petunia as a nanny, even though Gus complained about her incessantly. She seemed more of a fixture in the house, like the grandfather clock in their hallway that chimed every hour. May had forgotten long ago that Petunia, along with her other duties managing the house, was actually there to watch over her, a thought that now annoyed her slightly.

May's mother stopped to look at her then sighed deeply.

"May, maybe I've sheltered you for too long. With the long hours I work, I always really worried about you. It's not that you've ever given me reason to worry. You've been perfect. It's just that you are my baby and I'm…"

Reiko paused uncomfortably.

"I'm having trouble letting go. Phew. I said it. I had to pay a psychologist a fair bit of money to get those words out."

"You went to a psychologist to talk about me?" said May, shocked.

"Well, not exactly. I didn't seek one out. I went through some leadership training with a company psychologist and it all just came out. Then I booked a psychologist on my own for a few more sessions. The problem is me, not you. I'm having trouble *letting go*. Did I mention that?" She sounded nervous.

"Anyway, you don't need a nanny anymore. I have to trust you at your age. And I need to give you your space."

The last words sounded rehearsed.

"It all works out fine because I would have hated to have to let Petunia go," she added.

"What about all her stuff?" asked May.

"I'll have most of it shipped, but she's coming back to Canada at the end of the summer to get the rest of her belongings."

They continued walking in silence until they arrived at Auntie Bart's doorstep.

"We can talk about this more later," said Reiko. "I was thinking we can do some touring tomorrow before the evening performance since you're not in the play."

May cast a rueful smile her mother's way, which Reiko quickly interpreted.

"Unless you have other plans, of course," she said. "That

would be all right, too."

"I think I'll go the Globe with Chet to help out tomorrow," said May. "I mean, if you're really okay with that."

May wasn't even sure what time they would be allowed into the Globe but wanted to keep her day open just in case.

"Sure, honey. Whatever you like," said Reiko, looking slightly disappointed.

May wished her mother a good night and went upstairs where she found Chet playing guitar in his room.

"What happened at Hammer Dog's? Has he seen Sid?"

"No."

"Do you think we should tell him the truth, Chet? Maybe he can talk to Sid."

"I did."

"Really? What did you say?"

"I said that I thought Sid might be in trouble and asked him to warn him not to go to the Globe tomorrow. I wasn't sure what else to say. He seemed really concerned."

"Sid could be in jail for all we know after my phone call to Darwin today," said May.

"He's definitely not in jail."

"How do you know?"

"Because Hammer Dog told me he is staying with his mother tonight."

"His mother?" May still found it peculiar that Sid even had a mother. He seemed like some strange, otherworldly, abandoned character from a Dickens novel.

"I was surprised as well. He rarely mentions her. Hammer Dog just said she was in town and that he would go over to talk to her and Sid tonight."

"Let's hope he can talk some sense into him," said May.

"Let's hope."

May pulled out her father's phone that night and started researching environmentalism. She spent a couple hours reading as much as she could on nature conservation and various protection movements, trying to stay awake through her fatigue. She felt a sense of dismay at the breadth of the problems from pollution and deforestation to overfishing and she wondered whether anything could be done to reverse the damage. She thought about the company that was producing harmful products and about Sid's cousin, who was just doing his job as a farmer. With a heavy heart, she turned off her father's phone and went to sleep.

Just over an hour later, the alarm set for 1:00 a.m. buzzed in May's ear, waking her up disoriented and tired. Her room was pitch black as she sat up and tried to get her bearings. She opened her bedroom door and peeked out to see if there were any lights on in the house but everything was dark. She slipped out of her pyjamas and grabbed a folded shirt that was sitting on a chair, which she could barely make out in the shadows. She slipped the shirt over her head before throwing on her pullover jacket that was hanging on the door. She crept downstairs, strategically navigating the creaky steps, then snuck out the front door. The evening air was crisp and the wind was blowing the leaves on the street ominously. It was a cloudy night, making it particularly dark and dreary. May shivered and crossed her arms to keep warm. She walked briskly down the street until she reached the main intersection. The streets were deadly quiet and she waited several minutes before hailing down a cab. She calculated that the money Gus had given her would be enough to get to the Meeting Room and back. She stepped into the cab and provided the driver with the address. May noticed a momentary hesitation before he turned around and stepped on the gas. The driver kept looking back at her in the rear-view mirror, as if assessing something. After driving steadily for almost fifteen minutes, the neighbourhoods started to look very different. The houses looked either decrepit or abandoned and May started to get nervous. By this point, the cab driver was looking at her intently through the rear-view mirror as he slowed down in front of an old boarded up building.

"Are you sure you want me to let you off here?" May looked at the deserted street and the decrepit building and felt her pulse racing. She wasn't sure whether she should get out of the car or just have the cab driver take her home.

"Have you been to the Meeting Room before?" he asked suddenly.

"You know about the Meeting Room?"

"I work the night shift. I've picked up a few interesting characters from here before."

"No, it is my first time."

"You don't seem like the type, actually. But hey."

May paid the cab driver the money and opened the door reluctantly to get out.

"Wait," said the driver. "If you need a lift home, call me."

He handed her a card with his number on it.

"Thanks," said May.

"The entrance is at the back."

"Okay."

As the cab driver pulled away she looked at the abandon road and buildings apprehensively and let out an uneasy sigh. She walked around to the back of the building where it was intensely dark and where May's apprehension started to turn into panic. She tried to open the first of three graffiti-strewn doors, and it was locked. She walked to the second door and it had a large padlock on it.

She heard footsteps behind her coming around the building and she looked for a place to hide but the area was completely open. She stood in front of the padlocked door, terrified and unable to move.

The first thing May saw was two large high heeled black boots. They were attached to a very tall, skinny girl who emerged from the shadows wearing a short black studded skirt and a black leather jacket strewn with zippers. As she approached, she stopped and looked at May. She had short bangs and a short black straight bob, heavy green lipstick, and studs in her lips.

"It's usually the last door," she said, staring at May somewhat suspiciously.

"Thanks."

"First time?" she said, looking May up and down.

"Yeah," said May, suddenly feeling self-conscious about her sporty jacket.

"Follow me."

On the other side of the last door was an old staircase with a yellow light bulb hanging from a solitary wire. At the bottom of the stairs was a long hallway at the end of which was another black door. The girl approached the door and pounded on it with the side of her fist. May could hear music streaming through from other side. A large bald man with a tartan kilt on and a sleeveless leather jacket opened the door.

"Hello, Bo. Come on in," he said before stepping in front of May authoritatively.

"Who are you?"

"She's with me," said Bo.

The man hesitated for a moment before summoning them into a dark, smoky room with black painted walls and a small stage in the corner where a band was playing. The place smelled like urine and sweat and felt uncomfortably hot.

"Thank you."

"No problem. I'm Bo. You are?"

"I'm May."

The sweltering room was becoming oppressive and May quickly removed her jacket. She could feel the pit of her stomach drop when she looked down at what she was wearing. She had mistakenly grabbed Auntie Bart's swamp-green shirt with brown flowers on it. It was hideous. Bo looked down at the shirt then back up at May seriously.

"Whoa. That shirt is pretty atonal."

"Thanks," replied May, somehow ascertaining that for Bo, *atonal* was actually a nod of approval.

"I like what you are wearing as well. It is really dissonant," she replied, picking up on the music theme.

Bo's face lit up at what she obviously considered a compliment.

"Thanks," she said. "Let's move up to the front. I love this band."

They squeezed through the crowd as people hopped up and

down and bounced against each other in a somewhat vicious manner. When May looked up at the stage, she felt her chest contract violently. Sid was onstage with a guitar in his hand, singing with abandon. His hair was spiked and he had dark eyeliner and black lipstick on. When they got close to the front, Bo started hopping up and down to the music. May stood beside her, unable to move. The music was deafeningly loud and raw and eventually May felt her body start to lurch unintentionally.

Bo leaned in close to her ear and said, "I just saw some friends. I'll be back to check on you later. Stay away from the mosh pit if it's your first time. You could get hurt."

When Bo left, May stepped back away from the more aggressive dancing and watched Sid, mesmerized. When the band's set was over, Sid hopped down from the stage and was immediately surrounded by several people.

May stood immobile for a long time watching him work the room. As he got closer, she thought about slipping away but she knew she couldn't. Her heart began to pound uncontrollably as he got closer to her and she could feel her legs start shaking. Then suddenly he was standing in front of her. He looked at her blankly at first, as if he couldn't place her or didn't know who she was.

"May?" he said gravely. "What are you doing here?"

"Looking for a good punk band. Same as everyone else," she replied, realizing at that moment that Gus had either finally rubbed off on her or that she had somehow turned into a completely new species somewhere over the Atlantic Ocean.

Before Sid could reply, a man's voice came through a microphone on the stage and the crowd became really quiet.

"Good evening everyone," he said. "Thank you for coming."

There was a cheer from the crowd.

"We're here because the establishment is corrupt. Because greed is wrong. Because the fat cats will poison you, even kill you, to make a profit off of you."

Another cheer.

"And they need to pay."

Fervent cheers.

"And we're going to make them pay."

May was almost knocked over by the rowdy crowd who was screaming and jumping up and down.

"Let's get out of here," said Sid.

He put his arm around her firmly and escorted her through the back door, nodding to the doorman on the way out.

The cold air was a relief and May breathed it in deeply. Sid brought her around to the front of the building, where the street was ominously quiet. He started to say something but May reached up and put her finger over his mouth to signal for him to keep quiet.

"Can I borrow your jacket for a second? I'm cold," she said.

"Of course," he said, looking slightly puzzled.

He took his jacket off and offered to put it on May but she shook her head and stopped him. He watched her closely as she started feeling around the inside of the jacket. Underneath the flap of the pocket was a small device that felt a little like a metal button. She ripped it off his jacket, taking some material with it and held it out for Sid to see. He nodded in disbelief and took it from her. He dropped it on the pavement and squished it under his heavy boot, then he looked up at her inquisitively.

"Hannah put it there to get information about you for Koole. She said it was a GPS but it occurred to me it might be a microphone as well."

"You can end up in a lot of trouble for telling me that. There had better not be another device on me."

"There is one in your guitar case."

Sid stared at her for a long moment.

"How did you even find this place?"

"An MI5 agent called Darwin Lee had your name and this place in her notebook. Sid, I think you are in trouble. I wanted to warn you."

"You need to stay out of this. I don't want you involved."

"It is too late for that."

"I'm sorry about that. I didn't mean to implicate you in all of this. But thank you for coming here to let me know."

"Can we go back in now? I would like to listen to what Diego has to say. I presume that was Diego?"

"Yes, that was Diego. He never says anything of consequence at these events. He only shares important things with those close him."

"And you're close to this guy?"

"Yes."

"I see."

Sid looked affronted by the doubtful look on May's face.

"He's wearing a Hermès scarf," she said.

"What?"

"Hermès is a designer brand."

"I know what Hermès is."

"It's a thousand-dollar scarf. My uncle has one. My aunt freaked out when he bought it. Midlife crises. It doesn't seem consistent with his anti-establishment message."

"Diego's family has money. Maybe it was a gift."

"Aren't you environmental anarchists supposed to be more hippie-like? He sounds like a sleazy politician."

"May, I think you should get out of here. How about I call you a cab?"

"I can call one myself."

May pulled out the cab driver's number and started dialing when Sid grabbed her phone and hung it up.

"Actually, wait. Don't go yet," he said, looking conflicted before his face softened. "I'm sorry about the other day. I shouldn't have lost my temper with you."

"That's okay."

He put his hand on her cheek, looking regretful.

"I can't believe you're here. That you would risk…" Sid paused.

"I didn't only come to warn you, Sid. I came to ask you a question."

Sid looked at her intently, waiting.

"Was that you at the Globe today underneath the stage?"

"You really need to stay out of this."

"Answer the question," she said, surprised by her assertiveness.

"I was checking on some costumes and props underneath the stage."

"That is…how would you English say it? Rubbish? Bollocks? Sid, my family is going to be at the Globe tomorrow. I need to know they are going to be safe."

"Do you think I'm some sort of monster?"

"I am hoping you are not but I need to know that nothing is going to happen tomorrow night. The Queen is going to be there."

"The Queen will be fine. And I would never hurt anyone…intentionally."

"What's that supposed to mean? That if something happens to an innocent bystander, that's okay? Like someone being injured, or God forbid something worse, is justifiable? Think about what you're saying. Why are you doing this? There are better things you can do to bring awareness to the cause without destruction."

"You don't understand."

"Try me."

"You think if you stand around protesting with picket signs you can stop these people? You're so…"

"What? Naïve? That's where you are mistaken. *You* are naïve, Sid. You think Diego took you under his wing because you write great punk songs about anarchy."

"I think he appreciates that anarchy is a part of our message against these companies."

"Oh, of course. An anarchist with a Hermès scarf," she said sarcastically. "He knew you were vulnerable because of your cousin's death. He is brainwashing you into thinking this is the only way."

"Is that what you think of me? That I'm just some weak guy who can be brainwashed?"

"No. I am saying you are vulnerable. And he is taking

advantage of you."

"Oh, and do you have any other suggestions on how to stop companies that put dangerous agents into products just to make a profit—knowing full well those agents are harmful to people?"

"Are those the same people who you know might get hurt with your eco-terrorist acts?"

"Eco-terrorist? That's kind of a strong word."

"It's an accurate word. And yes. I do have a better suggestion. Go to law school and fight them legally. Crush them if you have to."

Sid looked surprised for a second but didn't respond.

May felt a lump in her throat forming. She had never given such an impassioned speech. She had never argued with anyone. She had always just observed. But this was more important than her fear. The Queen was more important. Sid was more important.

Sid continued to stare at her with his piercing blue eyes. He hesitated for a moment then took a step toward her. Placing his hands on her waist, he pushed her gently up against the cold building and kissed her deeply and urgently. May could barely breathe. It took her a few seconds to respond to him. When she let go and kissed him back he placed his hand at the back of her head and kissed her harder. Everything shut down in her brain those few moments as if she'd forgotten who he was and why she was there. She only came to her senses when she heard the sound of a car driving by and pulled away from him, catching her breath. He put his hand on her cheek then looked down at Auntie Bart's flowered shirt.

"Now that's anti-establishment."

They both burst out laughing.

"I like it," he smiled. "It is very…"

"Atonal?"

"Something like that," he chuckled. "You look very pretty, actually. Aside from my black lipstick all over your face."

"Sid, I need to go," she said dialling the cab driver's number.

"I know."

"Promise me nothing will happen tomorrow night."

"May, I know you have no reason to trust me. But please trust me."

"You need to think of a better way. You're going to end up in jail. Then you won't be helping anyone. You'll just be a criminal. And I'm sure Mr. Hermès-scarf-wearer won't give it a second thought."

Sid pulled May into a hug and rested his cheek on top of her head until the cab pulled up a few minutes later. He kissed her on the cheek and opened the door for her. As she climbed in, she turned back to him and said, "You should call Chet. He's worried about you."

*　　*　　*

The following morning was beautiful and warm, and the sunshine pouring in through the window of May's room woke her up with its light and warmth. She was surprised to see it was eleven and quickly ran downstairs to find Chet, who was sitting at the kitchen table eating a scone.

"I really slept in," said May.

"You must finally be feeling the jet lag."

"Your mum just left to go out with Petunia and Auntie Bart. She said she'd meet us later."

May sat down beside Chet and helped herself to a scone. "What time should we head out?"

"Since we can't get into the theatre until later, maybe we can go to Hannah's. She asked us to come over for tea. She spoke to Koole again and didn't want to talk to me about it over the phone."

"Sounds like she just wants to see you," said May.

"She's lucky I'm still talking to her."

"Are you sure you don't want to go alone so you can kiss and make up?"

Chet gave May a gloomy look, and she smiled widely back at him.

"She asked you to come too," he said.

"Well, maybe she wants a chaperone," laughed May.

"You're hilarious," he said, trying to suppress a smile.

May was feeling particularly calm and cheerful after seeing Sid the previous night. Her anxieties about the Queen being in danger and the Globe being blown up had subsided. May took a quick shower then put on a pair of shorts and a T-shirt. She stuffed a summer dress and a pair of shoes for the evening performance into her backpack. She was sure the dress would be creased by the evening, but she'd figure that out later. May left Reiko a note with the tickets to the show on the kitchen table, then drew a quick map of the area surrounding the Globe, with a big X on the spot where they should meet before the performance. She impressed herself with her knowledge of that area of London and smiled as she left the note on the table.

They arrived at Hannah's after what seemed like ages. May noticed for the first time how long the Tube ride took to get from the East End to the West.

Hannah answered the door herself this time and led them to the top-floor patio. They took an elevator up, which May hadn't noticed before, and which Hannah explained was broken the last time they had been there. Hannah hobbled more quickly on her injured leg and seemed glad to see them, offering them tea, sandwiches, and chocolates as May and Chet sat on a couch.

After they'd helped themselves to tea and snacks, Chet said in a very impersonal tone, as if he were only there on business, "So what did Koole have to say?"

Hannah took a deep breath. "Well, let me first say that some people have absolutely no breeding whatsoever. I thought he would never leave and he ate everything that was put in front of him like a complete barbarian, which I don't understand because he's actually from a good family. It just goes to show…" she trailed off.

"It just goes to show what exactly?" said Chet, his mouth full of chocolate.

"Never mind," said Hannah, looking uncomfortable.

"These are good chocolates, by the way," said May, trying to defuse the tension.

"Of course they are. They're Belgian," responded Hannah matter-of-factly.

"So what did Koole say, Hannah?" asked May.

"And what did you do to pay him this time?" added Chet in a disgruntled tone.

"I asked him over for dinner this time. I told him I found the fact that he was working for British Intelligence really sexy. I made sure my mother was home so he couldn't try any funny business. I can be quite shrewd when I want to be. I think I'd make a pretty good intelligence agent myself."

Chet looked repulsed and May put her hand on his shoulder to calm him down.

"I got him to talk some more. He said that he was going to be a part of a sting operation tonight at the Globe. He and several people who work for Diego will be arrested tonight. He couldn't divulge the plan but it will all be over before anyone gets to the theatre. Swift and covert."

"Covert apart from the fact that he told you, and you told us, and by this time half of London probably knows," said Chet.

May was shocked at the news and wondered whether Sid would be one of those arrested.

"Did he say anything else?" ask Chet.

"No, that's about it."

"If that's it, we'll be going," said Chet.

Chet got up and reached for his backpack.

"Thanks for information, Hannah," he said curtly. "And thanks for your hospitality."

"Do you have to leave so soon? Where are you going? I have more chocolates," said Hannah.

May, feeling a little sorry for her, gave her an apologetic look. As she got up to follow Chet to the door, Hannah said, "May, can I speak with you for a moment?"

The last time Hannah had asked to speak with May, she had

told her that she was no longer in the play. May wondered what bad news she'd bear this time.

"I'll meet you outside, May," said Chet, looking at Hannah suspiciously.

When Chet left the room, Hannah said, "You're not wearing those shorts to the party tonight, I hope."

May looked down at her shorts and t-shirt and said, "No, I brought a dress."

"Let's see it," Hannah demanded.

"What? Why? Is this what you wanted to talk to me about?" said May, suddenly feeling self-conscious.

"I won't have that Blanche Wilde thinking that she's so wonderful playing Ophelia. You'll have to look better than she does."

"You mean Tucker's sister? Hannah, I really don't care. I'm sure she doesn't care either."

"Oh, she cares. Trust me. The whole family cares. I'm just trying to help you not *embarrass* yourself."

"*Embarrass* myself?"

"I can lend you a nice dress," said Hannah.

"I'm fine, Hannah. I don't need to have a nice dress on to have dignity. But thanks anyway."

May left Hannah's very annoyed and slightly offended, but as she and Chet made their way over to the theatre, she opened her bag to look at the cotton sundress she had stuffed into it. What had looked appropriate that morning suddenly looked painfully inadequate.

She quickly forgot about her fashion woes when they arrived at the Globe. There were twice as many security people as the previous day, and the whole place was surrounded by a variety of people who were preparing for the Queen's arrival. There were people from the press, including photographers and TV crews, and onlookers surrounding the theatre. May had not expected such a commotion and began to feel extremely relieved she was going to be a spectator. She and Chet showed their security passes, entered the theatre, and headed toward the tiring house, where there was another sort of commotion.

Makeup artists, costume people, and several students were running around nervously. Willoughby was wearing the same handkerchief as the previous day and was waiting to get his makeup done, looking frustrated.

"That makeup artist is leaving my makeup until last," complained Willoughby. "I heard her say I was difficult! Can you believe that?"

"Do you really need makeup?" asked May.

"Of course! The lighting washes you out," said Willoughby.

"Why don't I start putting it on for you?" offered May, anxious to keep her mind off things. She didn't wear a lot of makeup herself but had, like most sixteen-year-old girls, spent an inordinate amount of time watching makeup videos and experimenting with it in front of the bathroom mirror. She had no experience, however, with stage makeup, so she asked the makeup artist, who was busy with Tucker's sister, if she could start doing Willoughby's makeup while he waited. May figured she wouldn't let a student do Willoughby's makeup if she didn't find him so objectionable. She handed May some brushes, creams, and powders and quickly told her what to blend and how to apply it. May returned with her arsenal of makeup and told Willoughby to keep his eyes closed while she applied dabs of colour to his face before rubbing it in. As May blended some cream into his cheek he said, "You have really soft hands."

"Oh, that's the sponge I'm using," said May.

"You smell really nice as well. What kind of perfume are you wearing?"

"I'm not wearing any. Maybe it's my shampoo," she said, embarrassed.

She was glad Willoughby's eyes were closed, because she was sure she was completely flushed. Willoughby was silent after that, which made May feel even more uncomfortable and she was glad to see the makeup artist, who had finally come to take over.

"I had better get going," said May. "I have to meet my mother. Good luck, Willoughby. Break a leg, as they say."

"Thanks, May."

May spotted several students, including Chet, who were peeking through the stage doors and waving to people they knew. May joined him and the two of them peeked out into the stands, which were now quickly filling up. Two girls behind them were giggling and talking loudly about how they had just snuck into the crowd to get an autograph from Penelope Flowerz for their parents, who would be thrilled.

May and Chet looked at each other, surprised.

"Penelope Flowerz is here tonight?" said Chet.

"Agent Lee said they were investigating possible threats to the Queen when we were at Windsor Castle. She never mentioned Penelope Flowerz. I think I should call her."

May pulled out her phone and dialed Darwin's number, and she picked up and said, "Are you at the Globe Theatre?"

"Yes," replied May.

"There are scanners and bugs all over the building. I'd rather talk in person. Meet me in front of the education centre."

"I'll be right there."

May left Chet backstage and walked through the main lobby to the education desk, where she spotted the agent.

"What can I do for you, Ms. Abbott?"

"Did you know that Penelope Flowerz is here?"

May knew the answer as soon as the question came out of her mouth because Darwin froze, looking stunned.

"That's not possible. Did you see her yourself?"

"I actually have no clue what she looks like but I heard some students say that they got her autograph for their parents."

"You've never seen Penelope Flowerz? Do you not get her show in Canada?"

"Yes we do but I don't watch gardening shows. I'm sixteen."

Darwin sighed.

"I have to go meet my mother. Is there anything else I can do?" said May.

"No, go ahead. Thanks for the information."

CHAPTER 16

May changed into her cotton dress, which wasn't as creased as she feared, and walked out of the main gates to meet her mother, Auntie Bart, Bedrich and Petunia at the appointed place, then ushered them to their seats and stayed with them until the play began. Everyone stood as the Queen arrived at the last minute, and that was May's cue to go back to the tiring house to see what was going on. She had told her mother that she would be helping out backstage, which wasn't true, because there was really nothing to do. She was just feeling restless after the news about Penelope Flowerz and wanted the freedom to be able to move around. Sid's words about the Queen being safe started to rush back. Were they targeting Penelope Flowerz? Had Sid been arrested before the play? She showed the security guard her pass, but he recognized her and let her into the tiring house without even looking at it. As she walked in, she heard the audience applaud as the play was introduced by the headmaster of the boy's school. Several girls dressed as courtiers waved to May silently as they tiptoed around awaiting their entrance. Chet was sitting near the stage doors listening to the action.

"What did Agent Lee say?"

"She was surprised. She was not expecting Penelope

Flowerz to be here tonight."

"That's not good news," he replied.

May wasn't sure why she hadn't told Chet about the previous evening and the fact that she had seen his best friend. He would have wondered why she had gone alone.

They sat quietly listening to the play which was going off without a hitch and the hour passed quickly. A large roar of applause came through the tiring house doors as the first half of the play came to a close. They couldn't believe sixty minutes had passed so quickly.

May and Chet got up and made room for the students who were exiting the stage.

"Chet, I'm going to go see if I can find my mom."

"I'll come with you."

As they walked toward the exit, they were met by two very large security guards in black suits who entered the tiring house purposefully. They had earpieces and started sweeping the room quietly and efficiently, as if they were searching for something. They ignored May and Chet, and when they had looked through the room for several minutes, one of them whispered something into a device on his wrist and walked back toward the door and opened it.

"Hello Ms. Abbott" said the woman who walked into the room.

May, recognizing the her, immediately curtsied and said, "Hello, Your Majesty. Nice to see you again."

"Twice in a week. Quite something. I see you are not performing tonight."

"No, things didn't work out, ma'am."

"These things happen."

"Of course, ma'am."

The Queen turned to Chet and said, "I wanted to say hello to the students in the play."

"I'm sure they'll appreciate that, Your Majesty," said Chet stepping aside as the Queen greeted the surprised students. Tucker looked radiant, interacting with the Queen as if she were an old friend. Professor Winterbottom looked positively drunk with what May suspected was either euphoria at the Queen's arrival, or something stronger, like the stuff in the little flask she carried around.

"What did you think of the first half?" said Willoughby, when he found May.

"It sounded great from back here."

"Oh. Were you not able to watch it from the audience?" he said looking slightly disappointed.

"Sorry Willoughby. I will watch the second half from the audience, I promise."

May wondered where Penelope Flowerz was and what was happening outside but no one was allowed in or out of the room while the Queen spoke to the students. After making the rounds, the Queen left the room with a very wobbly Winterbottom at her side. With only a few minutes left before the bell signaling the commencement of the second half, May realized it was too late to go find her mother. Students were running around touching up make-up and checking costumes. Tucker was pacing back and forth looking distressed.

"Do you know where Winterbottom went?" he asked May.

"Yes, I saw her leave with the Queen."

"She was acting really strange toward the end of the play."

"She did seem a bit loopy when she came off stage. I'll go see if I can find her, Tucker."

May walked down to the education centre but people were already taking their seats for the second half and she didn't spot the professor. As she started walking back towards the tiring house, a security guard put his hand on her shoulder.

"May Abbott?"

"Yes."

"Please follow me. Her Majesty would like a word with you."

The security guard escorted May to the Queen who was surrounded by a number of people. May approached inquisitively and curtsied. Queen Elizabeth looked around at the crowd as if trying to figure out how to secure some privacy. When it was obvious that this was not possible, she moved in closer to May and whispered, "I believe that there is some work to be done on the second floor of the tiring house. If you don't mind helping a friend of mine, I would be very grateful. You'll have to go there immediately. Please be discreet."

"Of course, Your Majesty."

May stood awkwardly waiting for further instructions but the Queen just gave her a little nodding nudge. May returned backstage where she found Tucker looking panic-stricken and infuriated.

"The beginning of the second half is just about to start. Where is Winterbottom?"

"I don't know," said May.

"She smelled a little like the floor cleaner they use for the toilets," added Chet.

"Isn't that her natural state?" laughed Willoughby.

"This is no time to joke, McGregor. She barely made it through the last scene. She was slurring her words. What do we do now?"

"Why don't you ask your dad? Maybe he can pay someone to think of a solution for you," retorted Willoughby.

Tucker shot Willoughby a dirty look and walked out the door to call two stewards into the room, demanding that they find Winterbottom immediately. The bell rang out, signally the end of intermission, and Tucker suddenly became exceedingly pale.

"We'll figure something out," said May.

"Why don't you play Gertrude, May?" implored Tucker.

By this time several students had gathered around and were looking at May.

"I don't know Gertrude's lines, Tucker. I can't help you here."

"Yeah, plus, what would your daddy say? Didn't he get her kicked out of the play to begin with?" said Willoughby snidely.

"Shut up, McGregor."

"Or what?" said Willoughby amusedly. "You'll pay someone to beat me up?"

Chet and Willoughby were arguing with Tucker and several

students chimed in to try to diffuse the situation. While Willoughby and Tucker continued to exchange words, May slipped upstairs discreetly and walked into the dark costume room. It seemed empty and quiet and she wondered what work the Queen wanted her to take care of when she saw a shadow moving behind one of the clothing racks.

"Professor Winterbottom? Is that you? Her Majesty said you needed help. Are you feeling okay?"

The shadow behind the clothing rack stopped moving.

"Professor Winterbottom is incapacitated," said an unfamiliar voice.

May peaked her head behind the clothing rack and found a tall, slender woman with blonde hair bedecked in sparkling jewelry and a long, elegant grey gown.

"What happened to Professor Winterbottom?"

"I sent her home in a cab. She wasn't in good shape. I was hoping I could replace her."

"Oh. Are you the Queen's friend?"

"I am."

"Do you know all the lines?"

"I sure do."

"I think they shortened it."

"I've done a lot of improv comedy so I am quick on my toes. I think I can handle it. But you need to make me look a little different than I do now. Perhaps you can help me get into costume?"

May looked at the woman suspiciously and wondered whether she was an eco-terrorist working for Diego. London was making her paranoid.

"I'm Penelope, by the way."

"I'm May."

"May...?"

"Yes. May," she said awkwardly.

"I see. I should have known by the Canadian accent."

"I don't understand," said May perplexed.

"It's a long story." she said eyeing May inquisitively. "You don't know who I am do you?" said the woman.

"Um….no." said May, thoroughly confused.

"That is actually refreshing," smiled the lady. "I'm Penelope Flowerz."

"You are kidding me."

"No. That's why we need to get this costume right so no one recognizes me. Will you help me? I'm almost finished my make-up. I'll choose a wig if you don't mind grabbing a dress."

"Of course," said May in disbelief.

"There are two dresses at the end of that rack that I am pretty sure will fit me. Do you want to do the honours?"

"Sure."

May pulled both dresses off the rack and assessed them.

"I'm so excited," said Penelope smiling widely. "You know, I sort of fell into the gardening show," she added as she wrestled a long brown wig into place. "Don't get me wrong, I am grateful for the success, but my first love has always been the stage. I adore Shakespeare. But no one would take me seriously on stage now. It's just the way it is. I've always dreamed about playing Shakespeare on the Globe stage."

"Well we'd better hurry up or they're going to cancel the play," said May removing a red dress from a hanger. "How's this?"

"It's perfect," smiled Penelope who was looking very different than she had a few minutes earlier.

"That wig and make-up make you look…."

"Like another person? That's what I'm aiming for. I took some make-up artistry classes when I was younger."

Penelope then slid behind a rack of clothing, threw on the red dress, and emerged looking triumphant.

"Wow. It looks fantastic," said May.

Penelope, suddenly looking serious, grabbed May's hands and held them tightly.

"May, thank you so much for your help. I am so pleased to have met you tonight."

"It was nice to meet you too, Ms. Flowerz." said May, feeling guilty for being annoyed with her in the past.

The two of them scurried down the stairs and ran right into

Tucker.

"Here she is," blurted May.

"Who in the name of goodness are you?" shrieked Tucker looking at the lady dressed as Gertrude.

"I'm the replacement actor for Ruth Winterbottom."

"Where are you from and how do I know you can even act? Winterbottom studied with the Royal Shakespeare Company when she was a young woman. We're supposed to be performing this play with a real actor," Tucker said disdainfully.

"Calm down, Tucker. Do not speak to her like that!" said May in a fiercely protective, almost threatening voice even she herself did not recognize, having never used it with anyone before. "This is my Aunt Petunia," she said, calming down slightly.

Chet shot May a confused look.

"She's a very famous stage actress in Canada," continued May.

"I don't care who she is as long as she knows Gertrude's lines and can act. I won't be made a fool of."

"Listen, there is no time to argue. The Queen is in the audience, so pull it together," said May.

At mention of the Queen, Tucker stood up taller, as if ready for any challenge.

"So you are sure she can act?" added Tucker speaking about Penelope in the third person as if she were in another room.

"She studied at the Royal Academy before moving to Canada. Trust me, Tucker."

"Okay, okay," said Tucker, suddenly looking appeased at hearing *Royal Academy*.

"Okay, Miss Petunia, this is an abbreviated version, so we've deleted a couple scenes and a few lines. I'll grab a script for you to look at quickly then you can review the rest between scenes. Just do your best and follow my lead," said Tucker. As he passed her the script he grumbled, "I can't believe we didn't have a back-up plan."

When Hamlet and Gertrude finally walked out onto the stage, May and Chet stood silently and stared after them for several seconds with looks of disbelief.

"Who was that…?" asked Chet.

"I don't want to mention her name here. I will tell you later," said May. "Maybe we should go watch a bit of the play. Willoughby is going to disown us as friends."

Chet looked at her completely perplexed as he followed her toward the exit.

As May reached for the door, it flew open and Sid burst into the room looking slightly frantic. He was wearing the black tailored suit which May thought made him looked striking and elegant, despite the fact that his hair was slightly disheveled. May and Chet just stood there stunned. Before Sid could say a word, Chet stepped menacingly toward him.

"What are you doing back here, Sid?"

A couple of students who were at the other end of the tiring house looked up, startled at the tone of Chet's voice.

"I'm looking for someone," said Sid.

"SHHHHHHH!" said one of the girls, pointing to the stage entrance.

Chet lowered his voice accordingly and said, "What's going on, Sid?"

"What's going on?" said Sid, looking infuriated. "Good question. Well, let's see. I heard that you had a chat with Hammer Dog last night. I also heard someone gave Koole information about a private conversation I had with a 'suspicious' blonde girl at the hospital. Was that you? Or did you get that little witch of yours, Hannah, to do your dirty work."

"Watch it, Sid," said Chet softly, but with of tinge of warning.

Sid leaned in closer to Chet angrily and said, "Did you know that Hannah had me tracked? Nice company she's been keeping. Koole is a dirty weasel. The two of them should make a great couple."

At this last comment, Chet stepped up to Sid and took a

swing at him, hitting him square in the jaw and knocking him over. May gasped, clasping her hand over her mouth. Sid's mouth was bleeding as he got up off the floor. Several girls stood up, startled, and one who was waiting to go on stage was gesturing feverishly toward the stage door to remind them that a play was going on as Sid push his way off the floor.

"Not bad," said Sid with a menacing grin. "But I'm sure you can do better than that … nice boy from Sheffield."

Chet took another swing at Sid and struck him in the stomach. Sid was hunched over for several seconds and looked like he was in pain. May stood there frozen, too shocked to move. Sid stumbled and gasped for air, looking a little winded, before he stood up slowly. He made no move to hit Chet back and gave him a disappointed look.

"I'm not going to fight you, Chet. I'm not the bad guy here. You're the one who's squealing on his best friend and listening to trouble-making drama queens like Hannah."

Chet took a third swing at Sid which landed on his right cheek, and May let out a small scream as Sid fell on the floor. She grabbed Chet's arm to restrain him and several girls who were waiting to go on stage came running. Sid got up off the floor, slowly this time, and started to stagger toward the door.

"I really have to go now, Chet. I'm a bit busy," he said as he stumbled out of the room, leaving a trail of blood from his cut lip on the wooden floor.

Chet's hand was bleeding and he was cradling it against his chest, staring blankly at the door. The girls slowly walked back to where they had been sitting before the incident. May stood paralyzed for several seconds, looking at the place where Sid had fallen to the floor. She quickly snapped out of her paralysis when she noticed Chet's wrist, which looked slightly twisted.

"Chet, just sit down and keep your hand stable. I'll see where he's going." But before she could leave, a security guard came into the room with Rae and walked over. The girl at the stage door was signaling to them to keep their voices down and the security guard complied, leaning in to speak closely and quietly to Chet and May.

"We're looking for someone. Have you seen anyone roaming around here?"

Chet seemed overcome by guilt and unsure of what he should do.

"What did he look like?" replied Chet.

"It's not a *he*, it's a *she*. A tall lady. Blonde," answered Rae.

"I haven't seen anyone," replied Chet.

"Okay, thanks," said Rae. "Let us know if you witness anything strange."

They left as quickly as they'd come and May turned to Chet.

"I think they are probably looking for Penelope Flowerz. I wonder if that is who Sid was looking for as well."

Chet shrugged, looking nauseously at his wrist, which was now swollen.

"Wait here, Chet. I'll be right back."

"I'm coming with you."

"But your hand. You need to see a doctor. It looks really twisted."

"It's fine. I'm not leaving now."

The area outside the theatre was quiet. There was security everywhere and they all looked extremely uncomfortable as if waiting for something to happen. Sid was nowhere in sight and nor was Darwin, so they walked around to the north entrance of the theatre and peeked through the doorway. Everything on stage looked like it was going as well as could be expected, and they stood absorbed for a few moments watching Gertrude. Chet was looking a little ill and squeezed into a bench to sit down with some fellow students but May remained standing at the entrance. She heard a commotion behind her where many of the security guards were gathered and saw Darwin approach the group anxiously looking frantic. May walked over to where she was standing and heard her say, "Subject Two is missing. Her bodyguards have informed us that they have not been able to find her for over 15 minutes."

Darwin looked both furious and terrified at the same time. She pointed at one of the security personnel and said, "Stop the play. Shut everything down immediately and lock down the building. Get Her Majesty out of here. You know the procedures."

"Wait!" said May. "Are you talking about Penelope Flowerz?"

Darwin turned and looked at May, surprised yet hopeful.

"Tell me you know where she is."

"Yes, I actually do. But can you recall the order to stop the play first."

"Ignore that last order. Stand by," said Darwin.

Darwin turned to May anxiously awaiting an explanation.

"You're not going to believe this one," said May.

"Try me."

May leaned over and whispered something in Darwin's ear.

Darwin staggered backwards almost losing her footing.

"How …?"

"It's a long story."

Darwin pulled May aside so they were out of earshot of the security contingent.

"We need to get her off that stage right now."

"No way, Agent Lee. This is a dream for her. Plus, it's the safest place for her, don't you think? No one knows it is her."

"I have to follow procedures."

"Not this time. If you stop the play, I will post that picture of you in a bikini that Jet Jango took. I swear."

"How did you….? You wouldn't dare."

May stared Darwin down in a manner she had never experienced before. Again, she was surprised at how good a poker face she could put on when it mattered because Darwin only glared back at her for a few seconds before relenting. She was seething at May but, still looking terrified, she spoke into a device that was on her wrist and said. "We have secured Subject Number Two."

"I'm going to watch the rest of the play now," said May.

"I'll come with you," said Darwin.

The two of them peeked through the curtain doors.

"Wow, she really is unrecognizable," whispered Darwin at one point.

May was surprised at how natural Penelope was on stage and how well the play was going considering the circumstance. When the play was over, they looked at each other and breathed a collective sigh of relief.

"I'll go help her out of her costume," said May.

"I'll join you in a few minutes."

May sprinted backstage and got there just in time to see the actors streaming into the tiring house looking relieved and thrilled at the performance. The audience continued to applaud as Tucker and his sister ran back out onto the stage for a bow. May disappeared into the back stairwell that lead to the third floor wardrobe as the crowd chanted *"Brilliant"* and *"Bravo."*

CHAPTER 17

When the students left the tiring house, May and Penelope Flowerz slipped stealthily downstairs where they were greeted by Darwin and two large security guards. They escorted Penelope out of the room and May and Darwin stood silently for several minutes.

"So did your sting operation go okay?" asked May.

"Yes, it was a success. We arrested almost everyone before the play started."

"Almost everyone?"

"Yes, we just arrested a couple more a few minutes ago."

May felt a pain in the pit of her stomach thinking about Sid.

"I presume Koole gave that confidential information about the sting operation to Hannah?" sneered Darwin. "He thinks he's becoming an MI5 agent. What a laugh."

"He certainly isn't very discreet."

"No, he's not. When we refused to lend him GPS tracking equipment, he purchased some devices online using his real name and address," she said rolling her eyes. "It doesn't matter. It was a successful evening despite his indiscretion."

"I'm glad everything went well for you," said May warming up to Darwin for the first time.

"Not everything went well. Penelope Flowerz' studio was destroyed this evening. You can read about it in the papers tomorrow."

"Was anyone hurt?"

"No. We knew it might be coming so we made sure the building was empty. We just didn't expect her to show up here tonight. I don't know what she was thinking."

"Did you get Diego?"

"Yes. we've been working on that one for a long time," said Darwin.

"Good for you."

"Well, I have to get going, Ms. Abbott. You're leaving tomorrow, I presume?" said Darwin.

"Yes."

"I'll be glad to have you out of the country."

"I'm going to miss you too, Agent Lee."

Darwin smiled at May.

"You helped us more than you're even aware, you know."

"Glad I could help," said May slightly confused.

"Have a safe trip back, Ms. Abbott."

"Thanks."

When Darwin left, May walked to where everyone was congregating in the piazza. As she strode through the crowd, she heard people commenting on the unknown Gertrude, debating the identity of Hamlet's mother. May started looking for her mother and Chet. She instead bumped into Hannah, who wobbled toward her furiously.

"There you are! I looked for you at intermission but the dressing room was blocked because of the Queen. Did you see her?"

"Just briefly," said May.

"Follow me. I brought some things for you," she said patting a large bag she held over her shoulder.

"Hannah, this isn't about what I'm wearing, is it?"

"Good Lord, of course it is. I brought everything for you. Just give me fifteen minutes."

Hannah didn't wait for an answer and hobbled purposefully toward the bathroom before May could object. She decided not to argue and just followed Hannah quietly. Perhaps some time away from the commotion might do her good. Hannah was true to her word, and fifteen minutes later, May came out of the ladies room looking glamorous in a designer dress, high-heeled black shoes, beautiful jewelry and a mysterious hair device that May couldn't see but was holding up her hair elegantly. Hannah had applied what she described as tasteful make-up, and May, hardly recognizing herself, couldn't believe how she'd been transformed so quickly. She thanked Hannah and they walked back to try to find everyone.

"I'm going to find my father. He's at the restaurant." said Hannah. "Make sure Tucker's sister sees you in that dress."

May rolled her eyes and chuckled, not believing anyone would care about such things. As she stood in the piazza looking through the crowd of people, someone grabbed her arm from behind. She turned around and found herself face-to-face with Sid. His hair was hanging over one eye and he still had dry blood on his lips. May stood speechless for several seconds.

"Sid, I thought you were ..."

"In jail?" he said.

May looked at him confused and he stared back at her intently.

"I guess that's understandable," he said.

May seemed to have lost her voice and just stood there staring at Sid as if he were a ghost.

"I heard you couldn't perform. I'm really sorry."

Before May could reply, Sid took two steps back and looked at her from head to toe.

"Wow. You look incredibly beautiful," he smiled.

"Uhhh, thanks," she said uncomfortably. She tried to snap herself out of her usual Sid-induced immobility. She needed to ask him what was going on, but all she could do was stand there speechless.

"How's Chet?" asked Sid.

"His wrist looks pretty sore."

"I hope so," he said dryly.

"It actually looks broken."

"Good."

A million questions were roaming through May's head but she didn't know where to start.

"I guess you're looking for some answers," he said reading her inquisitive look.

The crowd was thinning out and he pulled her into a corner discreetly.

"I can't talk about it right now but Chet was right. I was involved with some pretty radical stuff with Diego," he whispered. "Until they targeted my mum."

Before Sid's comment could register, May heard her mother calling her name rather loudly. She was navigating her way through the crowd, lifting her hand up every few steps so May wouldn't lose her.

"I'm so glad I found you," said Reiko, panting as she finally reached her. "We couldn't find you at the intermission."

May's mother glanced at Sid, eyeing his facial injuries suspiciously.

"Mom, you remember Sid, right?"

"Yes, of course. Hello, Sidney," said Reiko coolly.

"Hello, Mrs. Abbott," he said, reaching out and shaking Reiko's hand confidently. "If you'll excuse me, I need to go find someone," said Sid. "I'll catch up with you later, May."

May watched him walk away before turning back to her mother who said, "I got a glimpse of the Queen as she was leaving. Could you see her from backstage?"

"She actually came back stage at intermission, so I saw her up close then."

"That's what we thought!" said her mother excitedly. "Did she say anything?"

"Not much. She just said hello to everyone."

"How exciting," said her mother. "Petunia will be happy to hear that. Bedrich, Petunia and Auntie Bart are waiting near the front entrance. Why don't we head over there?"

When they reached the entrance, Bedrich handed May a bouquet of flowers and said, "Marvellous job. Simply marvellous!" He slapped May hard on the back as if she had hit a game-winning home run.

"Bedrich, for goodness sakes, May wasn't in the play," said Auntie Bart, throwing May an apologetic look.

"Wasn't in the play?" said Bedrich, looking confused.

"It's fine, Auntie Bart," said May. "Has anyone seen Chet?"

"I'm right here, May," said a voice beside her. Chet pulled her aside so they were slightly out of earshot and said, "Where on earth did you go at the end of the play?"

"Long story, Chet. I'll have to tell you another time."

Willoughby, followed closely by his mother and Hamish, squeezed through the throng of people before landing a spot next to May.

"You were so great, Willoughby!" said May, throwing her arms around him and giving him a hug. "You looked so comfortable up there. You're a natural performer."

"Thanks, May."

As Willoughby introduced his mother to everyone, May noticed a small commotion right next to them, where several people were gathering. Camera flashes went off and people were staring and whispering. May recognized the tall slender lady at the centre of the commotion. She was bedecked in sparkling jewelry and dressed in the long, elegant grey gown May had helped her change out of. The woman kept peeking over the crowd, staring in the direction of May's family. As the crowd around her grew bigger, the woman had to strain her head to maintain the connection with whatever she was looking at. May looked around, curious to know what her preoccupation was and found Sid at the other end of her gaze. He was standing right behind May with a roguish grin on his face.

"I'm back," he said, continuing to look toward the woman.

"You have a propensity for appearing out of nowhere," said May.

"Do I?" he smiled.

Sid turned his attention toward the tall blonde woman and with a subtle nod, he summoned her over. The crowd surrounding her parted to let her through and everyone turned their attention toward Sid. Petunia, Auntie Bart and Reiko, who were standing close by, had wondering looks on their faces as they closed in to see what was going on.

Sid put his arm around May and pulled her in toward the woman. "May, this is my mother, Penelope Beckensale."

Your mother?

May nodded, speechless and a little baffled. She reached out to shake Sid's mother's hand, but the woman ignored the hand, grabbed both of May's shoulders, and smiled at her fondly.

"It's so nice to meet you, dear," she said winking.

"It is nice to meet you too, Ms. Beckensale," reciprocating the discretion.

Sid, finally noticing Chet and Willoughby standing beside May, introduced them to his mother as well. She shook hands with both of them, stopping to put her hand fondly on Chet's cheek.

"It's so wonderful to finally meet you, Chet. Sid speaks so highly of you."

Auntie Bart and Petunia aggressively squeezed in closer to May like a couple of obsessed teenagers at a rock concert, and almost knocked her over. May, feeling embarrassed, felt obliged to make an introduction.

"This is Petunia and her sister Auntie Bart," she said, not worrying about explaining that she wasn't related to either of them. "This is Sid's mom, Penelope Beckensale."

"But…but...you're Penelope Flowerz!" cried Auntie Bart. "You're Sidney's mother?" she continued, sounding a little frantic.

"We thought Sidney didn't have any parents," said Petunia, not realizing how insensitive the comment was.

Penelope looked slightly hurt but said with dignity, "I'm very discreet when I visit Sidney. With the success of the show, I don't have a lot of privacy anymore and I thought he might be better off not being followed by the paparazzi all the time. Plus, Sidney always thought that people wouldn't take his music seriously if they knew I was his mother. Something about ruining his band's credibility."

She smiled at Sid fondly but he was having an intense

conversation with Chet. She turned her attention back to May and said, "I know you were supposed to be in the play tonight. I am so sorry that didn't work out."

May nodded and smiled, still having trouble processing the situation.

"And how are you liking London, May?" asked Penelope.

It was the first time anyone had asked her that question.

"I love it."

"I'm glad to hear that. How did you like the private pod on the London Eye? I booked it for a small event but my guests had to cancel at the last minute. Sid said it was a gorgeous evening. I'm glad he got to use it. It's not normally the sort of thing he would do."

That explained a lot.

"It was amazing. Thank you so much," said May. Sid and his mother had obviously talked about their evening.

Penelope chatted with everyone for several more minutes and was particularly cordial to Reiko. She even spoke to Hamish for several minutes, laughing at something he said. She signed autographs for everyone and wrote down a recipe for Auntie Bart and Penelope from one of her upcoming shows, which almost threw them both into hysterics.

Before Penelope left, she pulled May aside.

"I can't tell you how grateful I am for your help tonight, May. I have a lot to thank you for, my dear."

Before waiting for a reply, she turned and bade everyone goodbye, then left with the two large security guards who were waiting for her. Sid whispered to May that he was going to make sure his mother got out safely and he walked away briskly. Shortly thereafter, the students went downstairs to the party at the UnderGlobe. May pulled her mother aside and told her that she would be staying for the after-party and would go home with Chet later.

"But you have to pack for tomorrow's flight, May," Reiko protested.

"I know. I can do that tomorrow. The flight's late afternoon, right?"

May's mother nodded and sighed.

"Of course," said Reiko reluctantly. "Have fun."

"Thanks, Mom."

"Just be careful."

"I will."

"I can't believe how grown-up you look. Where did you get that outfit? That looks like a designer dress."

"One of the girls lent it to me."

"How nice of her. What a sweet girl."

May chuckled at the thought of someone referring to Hannah as sweet. "She has her moments," she said wryly.

CHAPTER 18

May walked down with Chet and Willoughby to the UnderGlobe, where a couple of hundred teens from the two schools had congregated and were mingling and dancing. The room was adorned with white balloons and flowers and lit up with numerous candles making everything look slightly enchanted. White tables and white couches made the space look elegant and chic giving the room a sleek, modern feel. The large oak tree in the middle of the room added a playful element and made the setting seem a little surreal. There was a DJ in front of a dance floor where students were already starting to gather.

Hannah was in a corner of the room speaking to a group of girls that May didn't recognize. When she saw May, she signaled that she would join them in a minute. Chet walked over to the food table and piled sweets onto a plate while Willoughby and May stood silently admiring the setting.

"Do you want to dance?" asked Willoughby.

"Maybe later, Willoughby. I was hoping to talk to Chet for a few minutes about Sid."

Noticing Willoughby's disappointed look, she said, "We'll dance later. I promise."

May noticed Hannah limping toward them as Chet

balanced a plates of brownies, cookies and other sweets with his uninjured hand.

Hannah looked at Chet's hand and said, "Wow. That looks pretty bad."

"He got into a fight," explained May.

"I heard," said Hannah.

"Everyone heard," added Willoughby.

Chet groaned and led them to a small, empty table, where the four of them sat with the plate of sweets.

"So what did Sid say to you?" asked May, unable to contain her curiosity.

"He apologized for shutting me out, and for not letting me know about his mother and everything else," said Chet, being discreet.

"Can you believe Penelope Flowerz is his mother?" interjected Hannah.

"Not really. Sid told me she had left her seat at the intermission but never returned," said Chet. "That's who he was looking for…"

"…when you gave him a beating?" said Hannah, looking greatly entertained.

Chet cringed slightly. "Don't remind me," he said. "I feel bad enough."

"You know, for a musician and an all-around gentle guy, it sure looks like you have quite a left jab," said May.

"He's from Sheffield. What do you expect?" said Hannah. "Scrappy."

"Yet artsy. Ahhh…the perfect man," said May with a mocking smirk.

"I like to think so," Chet grinned, winking.

Willoughby, who had been unusually quiet throughout the whole conversation, said, "Can we all just dance now?"

"I can't dance with this leg," complained Hannah.

"My brother played hockey with a broken leg once," said May. "You'll be fine. Let's go."

She dragged Hannah onto the dance floor and Chet and Willoughby followed, looking impressed by May's assertiveness. They danced most of the night, Hannah mostly swaying but looking like she was enjoying herself. May looked around several times for Sid but didn't see him, resigning herself to the fact that he had gone home with his mother. As the evening wore on, however, her disappointment grew and she wondered if she would see him again. At the end of the night, they made their way back upstairs to the piazza, where Hannah's father and Willoughby's mother were waiting at the Globe restaurant. May and Willoughby were well ahead of Chet, who was patiently waiting for Hannah to navigate the stairs. As May and Willoughby approached the table, May saw Hamish talking to Sid and the mysterious blonde girl they had seen at the hospital. She caught the last of what Hamish was saying to Sid in a serious and grave tone.

"I thought your mother and I connected on a very cerebral level. I could tell she thought I was witty and charming beyond my years, and I think she sensed how intrigued I was with her beauty, grace and style. But then it all went awry when she patted me on the head like I'm some sort of child."

"Oh, put a sock in it, Hamish," said Willoughby as he reached them.

Hamish ignored his brother and continued. "I'll have to wait until I'm older before she sees beyond this scrawny little child's body I'm trapped in. What would Samuel Beckett say? *I can't go on. I will go on.*"

"He would say that you're a git," said Willoughby.

Sid called May over to where he was sitting.

"May, this is my sister Gillian," said Sid.

"Hi," said May, reaching out to shake the girl's hand.

"Hi, May. It's nice to meet you. Sid, I'm outta here. You owe me," said Gillian with a look of exasperation toward Hamish, who was now talking to Willoughby.

"Thanks for keeping me company, Gill," Sid said gratefully.

May noticed everyone gathering around her and she realized it was time to say goodbye. The first to break the ice was Hannah's father, who said, "I hear you're leaving tomorrow, young lady. Have a safe trip back. You're welcome to stay with us if you ever come back."

May appreciated the sincere gesture and noticed that Hannah didn't cringe when her father gave her a hug. Instead she turned to May and said, "I'm not sure if I told you the other day, but I'm sorry about the play. I thought you might burst into tears when you found out and make a blubbering idiot of yourself, but I heard you handled yourself with dignity. I admire that. I don't think I would have been able to do that."

"Thanks, Hannah," said May, reaching over to give her a hug.

"I admire you too, May," said Hamish. "You're a credit to the English colonies."

Hannah turned to Hamish, lifting her crutch ominously close to his head and said, "Do you ever say anything that's not annoying or offensive?"

Hamish ignored the ominous crutch and gave May a hug. Willoughby and his mother followed suit, exchanging hugs and contact information. May waved goodbye to everyone and watched as they walked out through the piazza and onto the street.

Hannah kept looking back as she walked away, and May wondered what she was preoccupied with. Following Hannah's gaze, May found Chet talking to Sid's sister Gillian in a quiet corner. When the group had disappeared from view, she finally turned to Sid, who she found herself alone with.

"You're here. You stayed."

"Yes, of course I stayed. It's your last night."

"Why didn't you come to the party?"

"I had some debriefing with my new best friend Darwin Lee. She said she preferred I didn't go to the party."

"Really? So you've been waiting for me here all night? Why didn't you tell me? I would have left early," said May.

"That's why I didn't tell you," explained Sid. "I wanted you to stay and have fun with everyone on your last night."

"Thanks, Sid."

Sid smiled and said, "So can I take you home? My mother left me her car."

"Let me just talk to Chet."

Sid and May walked toward Gillian and Chet, who were sitting cozily facing each other and talking quietly. Gillian was looking intently at his wrist as if she was diagnosing it. Before May could say anything, Chet looked up and said, "Gillian has offered to drive me to the hospital."

He looked like he was intoxicated with what May thought might be a rather large crush.

"She is going to medical school next year. She thinks my wrist is broken. I will call you a cab, May."

"Actually, Chet, I am going to go home with Sid."

"Okay great."

"Chet, I'll fetch the car and pick you up on the street behind the building," said Gillian as she departed. "It was nice to meet you, May," she added as she walked through the main gate in front of the piazza.

When Gillian disappeared from view, Sid put his hand on Chet's shoulder and pulled him in close. "Gillian's four years older than you," he said.

"She mentioned that," replied Chet.

"She's also my sister," said Sid.

"I'm aware of that."

Sid let go of Chet's shoulder, and stepping away said, "I would have beaten you to a pulp had I fought back."

Chet smiled widely and said, "I know."

Sid turned to leave with May and said, "I'll see you at practice next week."

"See you at practice," said Chet.

CHAPTER 19

As Sid and May walked silently away from the Globe Theatre, there was a strange tension between the two of them that made May anxious. She had a million questions but wasn't sure which to ask first, or if she should ask anything at all. When they had walked for several minutes, Sid broke the silence.

"How was your evening?"

"Pretty strange," replied May. "You?"

"Pretty strange."

May instinctively glanced around to see if anyone was following them.

"Are you looking for someone, May?"

"Every time I'm with you, someone takes a photo of us."

"Only when we're kissing," laughed Sid.

"So you know about Jet Jango?" said May.

"Actually you and Jet are the reason I'm not in jail tonight."

"What do you mean?" asked May.

"It's kind of a long story. I don't know where to start."

"I'm not going anywhere," said May.

They arrived at the lot where Sid's car was parked and they both got in.

"I'll start at the beginning, I suppose," he said contemplatively. "My cousin died of cancer last year. We were really close."

"I know. Chet told me. I'm so sorry."

Sid started the car and pulled out of the lot.

"I was so angry. I thought people weren't taking environmental issues seriously enough. I truly believed that Diego and Griffin had methods that would eventually work."

"Who's Griffin?"

"He's the bloke who gave me that package at the demonstration I took you too."

"Right. The one with the orange and brown sweater. I remember him well. Darwin asked me about him."

"I'm sure she did."

Sid looked straight at the road with an earnest look on his face.

"I never intended to hurt anyone or put anyone in danger. I started having second thoughts when the lady was injured in the fire that Koole set. Then one day Diego approached me about targeting the Penelope Flowerz show. Of course I asked him not to do that."

"Did he know she was your mother?"

"He said he didn't, but I knew he was lying. My mother and I are discreet but Diego's a smart guy. He would have done his research on me. I think he was actually testing me. I never trusted him again after that."

"Was he targeting your mom because of that bad company that sponsors her show."

"Yes. I told Diego I had already spoken to my mum and she promised to drop the sponsorship. She was glad to part with the company but wouldn't have been able to break the contract immediately."

"I wonder whether he became close to you because he knew she was your mother."

"I've thought of that. He was always curious about my weekends in the Isle of Wight. He must have figured out that I was visiting her. He could keep track of where she was that way. He had his own agenda and was going to do whatever it took to see it through. He wasn't happy when I asked him to call off the demonstration at her studio. After that, he started keeping things from me which I found suspicious. I knew he was determined to make an example of her."

"Is that when you went to Darwin?"

"No. Actually Darwin came to me, thanks to you."

"I don't understand."

"Darwin knew Jet Jango was following me not only because he wanted Diego, but because he recently found out that Penelope Flowerz is my mother. He's been stalking her for years. He's a real tosser, that one."

"I heard," said May.

"But Darwin couldn't confiscate his camera unless she was sure that there was evidence of a crime on it. And Koole provided her with that after he met with Hannah on Tuesday night."

"So why is that thanks to me?"

"Chet told me that it was your idea to trust Hannah and tell her about the package that Griffin gave me at the demonstration."

"An obvious mistake! She wasn't trustworthy if she told Koole!"

"That's not the point. Your faith in people is what ultimately saved me."

"You mean my stupidity? My innocence?"

May cringed as the words left her mouth.

"That's not what I meant at all, May. And innocence is pretty underrated."

"So what did Darwin find on the camera?"

"Darwin found several recent pictures of Diego inspecting my mother's studio in great detail. She suspected that I was the reason that the protest Diego had planned for the show had been cancelled so she brought me in so she could see the look on my face when I saw the pictures."

"You were surprised, I presume."

"Very."

"So you cut a deal with her."

"Yes. She was planning on arresting me either last night at the Meeting Room or tonight at the Globe. She had a lot of stuff on me. But she knew that I could give her something she wouldn't otherwise have."

"Diego."

"She offered me full immunity if I agreed to testify against him."

"Just last night you said you were close to him."

"I was lying. I was just there so Diego wouldn't get suspicious. I knew by then that Diego was setting me up and that he was no friend of mine."

"So the plan at the Globe Theatre was just a diversion?"

"That's right. Diego had a plan for tonight which I was supposed to lead. All the people who were involve were people who I knew he didn't trust, including Koole. He set us all up. He knew the plan would never work with the amount of security tonight. Darwin had her suspicions as well. When Koole told Darwin about the plan, it didn't sound right to her. It seemed too elementary for something Diego would plan so she suspected he was trying to deflect attention from something else."

"A plan to destroy your mother's studio."

Sid nodded.

"Chet told me she's the person you were looking for during intermission when …"

"… he pummeled me? I'm sorry you had to see that. A little humiliating, honestly. But I really couldn't fight back. I couldn't risk getting detained by security."

"Why didn't you just tell Chet you were looking for her?"

"I didn't get the chance to tell him. I didn't think he would take a swing at me."

"You kind of provoked him with the comment about Hannah and Koole."

"Yeah maybe," he said. "To be fair to Chet, I've really shut him out lately. I know he was frustrated with me."

"Why did you bring your mother to the Globe in the first

place?"

"Oh I didn't. She was not supposed to even be in London tonight. But…."

Sid looked at May uncomfortably.

"You're not going to believe this one."

"Sid, I'm not sure anything would surprise me at this point."

"I think this might."

May looked at him, alarmed.

"My mum wanted to come to the play to see you."

"What?"

"She was incredibly curious to meet you, especially after a briefing from Darwin. Darwin must have said a lot of nice things about you."

"Imagine that."

"She swore to Darwin she would not even be in London tonight. MI5 provided extra security for her. Darwin wanted her as far from London as possible. I was on my way to the Isle of Wight to meet her when Darwin called to tell me she was at the Globe. We're not sure how she slipped by security. Darwin tried to convince her to leave but my mum refused, saying she wasn't going to let these kinds of people dictate her life. She admitted to me afterwards that it had nothing to do with anyone dictating her life. She really just wanted to see you. Of course she didn't know you were no longer in the play.

Anyway, I was called in to try and convince her to leave but by the time I got to the theatre, she was missing. She disappeared during the intermission. They had already arrested most people before the play began but they were alarmed when she went missing. Darwin was also worried about her presence at the Globe being posted online."

"I bet that happens everywhere she goes."

"It does. I still have no idea where she went. She wouldn't tell me. But it might have something to do with Professor Winterbottom. My mum told me when Winterbottom was speaking with the Queen she seemed intoxicated. I think my mother may have brought her home."

May didn't trust herself to respond so quickly changed the subject. "I wonder who ended up playing Gertrude."

"Everyone is wondering."

"I heard she was an actress from Canada," lied May, not betraying his mother's secret.

"I heard she was your Aunt Petunia," said Sid.

May laughed. "That's ridiculous."

"I thought so too," said Sid.

"I can't believe your mother is Penelope Flowerz. So that's why you know so much about plants and flowers, like you did in St. James Park."

"Mum's taught me a little about botany over the years."

Sid made a sharp turn and May recognized the street adjacent to Auntie Bart's.

"Sid, can I ask you a question?"

"You can ask me anything you want."

"What were you doing under the stage?"

"I can't tell you that, May. All I'll say is that I needed Diego and everyone else to think I was carrying out his plan."

"Was it the thing that Griffin gave you?"

"No, but it was something similar. Of course, Darwin's team removed it that night. The package I received from Griffin was for something else Diego was planning. I'm not supposed to talk about that either so I can't tell you much more. The second package Griffin gave me was a rare vodka from Russia that is not easily brought into the country because it's so strong it's on the 'dangerous liquids' list for Great Britain. Griffin was able to smuggle it in somehow. I bought it for Hammer Dog for all the extra lessons he's been giving me this year."

"Can I ask another question?"

"Of course."

"What were you doing at the hospital?"

"I was there to see my grandmother who hasn't been well."

"I'm sorry to hear that. What were you and your sister talking about ... if you don't mind me asking? You said you were going to take care of HRH?"

"Sid chuckled. That's what we call Gillian's twin sister, Georgia. She has always been the Queen of the house so Her Royal Highness is a moniker that's stuck over the years. She's been seeing some guy who is a bad influence. He asked her to give up her studies and move to America with him. We were planning on having a chat with her. More like an intervention. My mum and Gillian wanted to make sure I was there because they think I'm the only person Georgia ever listens to. Unfortunately, Georgia left for America last night. She and my mother had a row yesterday."

"Your sister also mentioned the police."

"They had been coming around my mother's house asking questions about me, before MI5 got involved in the case."

Sid glanced over at May and said, "I'm sorry I ignored you at the hospital."

"You seemed almost angry with me," said May regretting the comment immediately. She turned red, suddenly feeling embarrassed for sounding like a needy child.

"I wasn't. I was just confused. I ignored you because I didn't want to feel the way I was feeling. Ever since my cousin died, I've had this obsession with controlling everything. Not being able to control what I was feeling for you was a bit bewildering. I couldn't make any sense of it so I tried to ignore it."

Sid reached into his bag which was at May's feet. He pulled out a small box and handed it to May. She opened it and found a ring with a king's face etched into the top of it.

"A friend of my mother's is a well-known actress. This is a ring that she always wears before she goes on stage because she says it brings her luck. I asked her to lend it to me so I could give it to you before tonight's performance. Gill picked it up for me. My mother's friend said you could have it. I've been carrying it around but the moment was never right to give it to you. It's just a cheap prop ring."

May slipped it onto her finger.

"It fits perfectly. I love it. Thanks. That was very thoughtful of you."

Sid parked his car outside Chet's house and the two walked up to the door.

"So what will you do now, Sid?"

"Finish school and just lay low. My mum rented a house in London and asked me to live with her for a while, which I think I'll do. I know it didn't show tonight, but she's completely furious with me. Actually beyond furious. She said she was extremely disappointed."

"Ouch," said May.

"Let me tell you, the conversation I had to have with her when I cut a deal with Darwin wasn't a happy one. She suspected I might be into something because the police had been round to her house, but when she found out I was involved in a group that had destroyed property and harmed people, she was incredibly upset. I feel terrible that her studio was destroyed."

"I can't imagine. It's a harsh lesson."

"May, you were right about me being naïve. I couldn't say anything last night when we spoke at The Meeting Room but like I said, I knew by then that you were right about Diego. I couldn't believe you saw the truth about him in one glance. I couldn't see it that whole time."

"I'm sorry, Sid."

"Yeah. Me too. It's made me reassess everything. I am even thinking about law school."

'Really?"

"Yes. My father was a very well-respected barrister."

"He was?" said May trying not to look as surprised as she was.

"Yes. He went to Cambridge. That's why I was so surprised when you mentioned it last night. Maybe I will follow in his footsteps. It wasn't my original plan."

"Don't tell me. You were going to be a punk rocker."

"Something like that," he smirked.

"I'm sure Cambridge will be excited about an anarchist attending their school."

Sid laughed. "I spoke to my mum about it this morning and

she was thrilled I would even consider it. She has been amazing. She is negotiating hard with her network to stop advertising with any company she deems environmentally irresponsible and is still so supportive of me even after what has just happened. She has even offered to help me start my own environmental group."

"One that won't resort to destruction and violence?" said May dryly.

"Very funny, May," Sid chuckled.

"Well at least you get free home-made pastries and baked goods at your mom's house for the next little while," she said.

"She makes an amazing cup cake, that's for sure."

He suddenly looked slightly uncomfortable, as if waiting for some sort of cue from her.

"So what do you have left on your list?" he said changing the subject.

"I threw the list in the Thames," said May.

"I'm going to turn you in for polluting our waterways."

"There were tons of things left on the list. The National Gallery, the British Museum, the Courtald Gallery, the Victoria and Albert Museum…should I go on?"

"You have to come back."

"I think so too," said May.

"I'm sorry you're leaving tomorrow. I would have liked to have spent more time with you, May. You're different than most of the girls I've gone out with in the past."

"What kinds of girls have you gone out with in the past? Terrorists, pickpockets, thieves?" asked May playfully.

"I've dated a lot of different types but you're much more…" he paused, as if looking for the right adjective to describe her.

Do not say innocent.

Sid took a deep breath, looked at her with a fond smile said, "Self-assured."

May heaved a sigh of relief.

Sid moved in closer to her and put his arms around her waist.

"Can I please kiss you now?"

"Since when have you ever asked?"

He kissed her much more gently and affectionately than he had the last time. His lips and skin felt softer and he held her close while is hands traversed up and down her back. They stood in front of the dark house for what May calculated the next day was close to half hour before she was finally able to tear herself away from him.

"I should go in Sid. It's really late."

He kissed her forehead and her cheek and held her face in his hands gently. "I'm really going to miss you."

"Me too," she said.

"I'll see you around then, May."

"See you around, Sid."

He gave her a final kiss and May watched him walk down the front path and onto the street. They had not talked about getting in touch with each other, but somehow it didn't matter at the moment. She would think of that later.

When he disappeared, she stared at the street after him for several minutes, savouring the cool, blossom-filled evening air. The lights in the house were out, but when she went inside, Chet was reading on his computer in the sitting room waiting up for her.

"Let's go sit out back for a few minutes," he said. "It's your last night and it's a beautiful evening."

"It's a little chilly," said May.

"Not at the back. It's sheltered. Come on."

A few minutes turned into a few hours as they recounted the events of the week, laughing and giggling as quietly as they could so as not to wake anyone. May finally told Chet about her evening at The Meeting Room and about Penelope Flowerz being the mystery Gertrude. Chet told May that Sid's sister had kissed him goodnight and he was seeing her again the following evening. Chet snuck into the house at one point and grabbed a present wrapped in red and white paper that looked like a candy cane.

"I bought you this. I hope it fits."

May opened the gift and found a red and white striped shirt

that matched the wrapping paper. It had a crest on it with two crossed swords.

"It's a Sheffield United jersey," explained Chet. "They're my football club."

"Wow. It's really...um...striped."

Chet laughed. "I know you probably won't wear it back home. I bought it for you so you'd come back and wear it to a match. I'd love you to see Sheffield. It's a great town."

"I love it. I will definitely wear it. And I will try to come back soon."

May was removing the tags on the shirt and was putting it over her head to try it on when Chet said softly, "May?"

"Yes, Chet."

"Can I asked you a question?"

"Of course, Chet. What is it?"

"Is your middle name really Bungo?" he said, breaking out into hysterics.

"Yes. Don't mention it!" she said.

"Sexy, May. Really sexy."

"Stop it!" she frowned. "You're worse than my brother. Gus used to threaten to tell everyone when I was younger."

"Well, I would threaten to tell the Queen, but it's obviously too late for that," he said as they both broke out into fits of laughter.

They talked until the dawn crept into the dark sky then they headed up to their rooms to catch whatever sleep they could. A few hours later Reiko peeked into the guest room.

"Did I wake you?"

"It's okay," said May.

"How was the party?"

"It was fun," said May, rubbing her eyes.

"I started packing for you."

"Thanks, Mom. I'll take care of the rest," said May. "What time do we have to leave?"

"The car will be here at four. Maybe I shouldn't have woken you, but Auntie Bart was making brunch."

"I'm glad you did. There's something I have to do."

May quickly stuffed whatever was unpacked into her suitcase and went downstairs. After a hasty bite, she told her mother she was going out for a while.

"Are you going out with Chet?" asked Reiko.

"Chet went to the library to study for an exam he has tomorrow morning," Auntie Bart cut in. "He left really early."

May looked at Auntie Bart, surprised. She and Chet had gone to bed at the crack of dawn, so he was probably exhausted.

"I just want to go out for a bit by myself before we leave. Is that okay?"

"Of course," replied Reiko reluctantly. "Don't go far."

"I won't," said May, grabbing a sweater and running out the door.

CHAPTER 20

A car arrived to take them to the airport at exactly four. Chet came down from his room as they were putting their bags into the trunk. He gave May a hug and said, "Safe trip, May. I'm going to miss you."

"I'm going to miss you too, Chet. Thanks for everything."

May slept most of the way back Toronto, having had very little sleep the previous night. In the customs line at Pearson Airport, May saw a woman reading a newspaper that had a story about Diego Taylor splashed all over the front page.

Reiko dropped off May and their luggage at their brick suburban home then left to run some errands. May walked into the family room, where she was greeted by Gus and a girl she did not recognize. Gus had a cast on his leg and was hobbling toward her.

"Hey, welcome back, May. This is Melody," he said, turning to the girl.

"Nice to meet you, Melody," said May dropping her bags in the hallway.

"I'm just going take Melody home," said Gus. "I'll be back in ten minutes."

May went up to her room, opened her suitcase on her bed and started throwing things into her laundry basket and hanging up things she hadn't worn. Near the bottom of her suitcase was a plastic bag she didn't recognize with a yellow sticky note on it that said, *"Hannah called and told me to put the dress and shoes in your suitcase. She said they looked better on you. I wasn't going to argue. Chet."*

May smiled. As she took Hannah's dress out of the bag and laid it on the bed, she heard her bedroom door swing open behind her.

"Nice of you to call me back from England, May."

"Was I supposed to have called you back? Sorry, Gus. It was kind of a crazy trip."

"So I gather," he said, looking at her curiously as he sat on the bed against some pillows and stuffed animals.

May continued putting things away without looking up. "I heard you won your hockey tournament," she said.

"Yeah, we won it with our back-up goalie."

"I know. Mom told me. I'm so sorry. How bad is the ankle?"

"Not as bad as last time."

"You should be proud, Gus. You got them to the finals."

"Yeah, I was really upset until the practice before the final. I was sitting in the stands and Melody sat beside me. She was watching her brother play. We're going out now."

"Wow. All with an injured foot. Well done."

"*Because* of an injured foot," he said, affectionately tapping the cast on his leg.

"Capitalizing on the sympathy factor, eh? That'll wear off."

Gus looked slightly pensive and said, "Actually, we really like each other. It's kind of serious."

May laughed. "I leave you alone for eight days and you're all in love now. I think I might barf."

Gus threw a pillow at May's head, which missed her left ear.

"Bad aim. I guess that's why you're a goalie and not a pitcher."

Gus realigned the pillows at his back and propped his injured foot up onto the bed.

"So did Zorro pass his test?" she asked, sitting down beside him.

"He's not taking it until next week," said Gus.

"So what are the responsibilities of Canadian citizenship?" asked May.

"I'm not the one taking the test. How should I know?" he said, smirking.

May rolled her eyes. "Weren't you helping him?"

"I only remember a couple," he said. "Respecting the rights and freedoms of others. Eliminating discrimination and injustice." Gus looked up at her impatiently and said, "So?"

"So what?" said May coyly.

"So I heard snippets of the trip from the conversation Dad was having with Mom on the phone last night but would like to get your version."

"I think my version might be slightly different than Mom's."

"Intriguing," he said, sitting up attentively. "Well, let's hear it."

"Before I tell you anything, I thought you'd be happy to know that on my last day in London, I went downtown by myself and got totally lost."

"You got lost? On the way to what?"

"On the way to nowhere. I just went downtown and walked up strange streets until I had absolutely no idea where I was."

Gus looked at May skeptically. "Are you joking?"

"No. Geez, Gus, was I that boring before I left?"

Gus laughed. "Do you really want me to answer that question?"

May let out a contemplative chuckle.

"So did you find anything interesting while you were lost?" asked Gus, looking at her intently.

"It was all interesting. Just walking around streets that weren't on the way to a particular destination was really fun. I found hidden laneways, hidden parks and little alleyways. Places where Londoners actually live. I felt like the city was revealing a different part of itself to me...like I was seeing a different layer of the city."

Gus looked at her with admiration. "Wow. That's sounds really cool, May."

"It was. Until I looked at the time and realized I was going to miss my flight. I had to ask someone where the nearest Tube station was. I arrived at Auntie Bart's five minutes before the taxi came to bring us to the airport. Mom looked like she was going to have a heart attack when I got back. She was completely frantic."

Gus laughed. "Classic."

May got up off her bed and reached for her bag.

"Can you drive the car with that broken foot?" she asked.

"Yes, I just drove Melody home. My driving foot is fine."

"Let's get out of the suburbs. We can drive into the city and grab some lunch somewhere so I can tell you about my trip," said May.

"You finally want to get out of the suburbs?" said Gus smiling widely. "May, I thought you'd never ask."

ABOUT THE AUTHOR

Jackie lives in Toronto and has two beautiful daughters. She has a weird obsession with all things England and dreams about very odd things like having a thatched roof and playing tennis with the Queen. She has watched the BBC version of Pride and Prejudice more than she would admit to any person of sound mind and often wonders why her mom didn't name her Elizabeth.

Printed in Great Britain
by Amazon